SLAVES OF TARNE

He moved closer to me and stroked his hand down the front of my chest. I drew in breath sharply.

'You like that, do you?' he said. His voice was quiet and sure.

'Yes,' I confessed.

He gave me a slap across the face. Not hard, but hard enough. His body was touching mine. He looked me straight in the eye.

'Yes, what?'

'Yes, sir,' I corrected myself. How he realised this was what I wanted I didn't know. It was more than I could have hoped for from him. With all my night-time fantasies, I had never once been able to experience more than a reluctant charade of domination. Now, that would all change. In a few hours I might be experiencing what I had always dreamt about. I could find myself in chains, aboard a slave ship, one of many being transported to spend our lives as the chattels of other men.

D1596966

SLAVES OF TARNE

Gordon Neale

First published in 1998 by
Idol
an imprint of Virgin Publishing Ltd
Thames Wharf Studios,
Rainville Road, London W6 9HT

ISBN 0 352 33273 5

Cover photograph by Colin Clarke Photography

Typeset by SetSystems Ltd, Saffron Walden, Essex
Printed and bound in Great Britain by
Mackays of Chatham PLC

SAFER SEX GUIDELINES

These books are sexual fantasies – in real life, everyone needs to think about safe sex.

While there have been major advances in the drug treatments for people with HIV and AIDS, there is still no cure for AIDS or a vaccine against HIV. Safe sex is still the only way of being sure of avoiding HIV sexually.

HIV can only be transmitted through blood, come and vaginal fluids (but no other body fluids) passing from one person (with HIV) into another person's bloodstream. It cannot get through healthy, undamaged skin. The only real risk of HIV is through anal sex without a condom – this accounts for almost all HIV transmissions between men.

Being safe
Even if you don't come inside someone, there is still a risk to both partners from blood (tiny cuts in the arse) and pre-come. Using strong condoms and water-based lubricant greatly reduces the risk of HIV. However, condoms can break or slip off, so:
* Make sure that condoms are stored away from hot or damp places.
* Check the expiry date – condoms have a limited life.
* Gently squeeze the air out of the tip.
* Check the condom is put on the right way up and unroll it down the erect cock.
* Use plenty of water-based lubricant (lube), up the arse and on the condom.
* While fucking, check occasionally to see the condom is still in one piece (you could also add more lube).
* When you withdraw, hold the condom tight to your cock as you pull out.

* Never re-use a condom or use the same condom with more than one person.
* If you're not used to condoms you might practise putting them on.
* Sex toys like dildos and plugs are safe. But if you're sharing them use a new condom each time or wash the toys well.

For the safest sex, make sure you use the strongest condoms, such as Durex Ultra Strong, Mates Super Strong, HT Specials and Rubberstuffers packs. Condoms are free in many STD (Sexually Transmitted Disease) clinics (sometimes called GUM clinics) and from many gay bars. It's also essential to use lots of water-based lube such as KY, Wet Stuff, Slik or Liquid Silk. Never use come as a lubricant.

Oral sex
Compared with fucking, sucking someone's cock is far safer. Swallowing come does not necessarily mean that HIV gets absorbed into the bloodstream. While a tiny fraction of cases of HIV infection have been linked to sucking, we know the risk is minimal. But certain factors increase the risk:
* Letting someone come in your mouth
* Throat infections such as gonorrhoea
* If you have cuts, sores or infections in your mouth and throat

So what is safe?
There are so many things you can do which are absolutely safe: wanking each other; rubbing your cocks against one another; kissing, sucking and licking all over the body; rimming – to name but a few.

If you're finding safe sex difficult, call a helpline or speak to someone you feel you can trust for support. The Terrence Higgins Trust Helpline, which is open from noon to 10pm every day, can be reached on 0171 242 1010.

Or, if you're in the United States, you can ring the Center for Disease Control toll free on 1 800 458 5231.

Prologue

A youth, thought Caspar, was no more than an ornament. He may be pleasant to look at. He may even be useful, or good to hold, but if he became damaged in some way you simply cast him aside and replaced him. Young men were not anything to lose sleep over.

It had occurred to him – only once, and then briefly – that if this rule could be applied to young men per se, then it should have followed that it could also be applied to himself. He dismissed this idea as soon as it entered his mind and refused to approach it ever again. After all, he was different. He was beautiful, but more than that: he was aristocratic. In Tarne, he was the acknowledged demagogue. If only men fucked each other on the mainland as they did in Illyria. They had done so in his great-grandfather's time. If that could be so now, Caspar could have claimed influence and power over many miles. Of course, it wasn't to be, at least not for the present. Tarne, and indeed Illyria itself, were small oases of male love amid a desert of prudish child-rearing.

The Illyrians still openly kept and sold captive men as slaves, but they had the good fortune to be living on an island and

1

therefore were not subject to the laws of the mainland. Tarne was merely a village and the community of which Caspar was the head was protected only by a high brick wall round the old mansion. This didn't worry Caspar. Indeed, those close to him had been more than a little concerned about his increasing recklessness.

Every year, on Orion's Night, the anniversary of his great-grandfather's passing, he made use of one of his boys in a ceremony. When he had first inherited Tarne, he had been content to let this rite be representational. His 'victims' – blond and smooth (as were all his slaves in contrast to the dark hirsuteness of himself and the other Superiors) – were happy to be bound to a stone altar and pleased to surrender their arses. They neither knew nor cared what this erotic humiliation was all about. They had come to Tarne willingly and were grateful to have their master's cock inside them. To be stripped naked, restrained and fucked was what they desired most. However, the delights of this tame play-acting soon palled for Caspar. The ceremonies became more of an ordeal for the unfortunates who were chosen to be at their centre. Rumours spread around Tarne, especially among those slaves who feared it might be their turn to be picked next. It was generally thought that Caspar was losing his grip on reality.

It was the year before Caspar was to meet Pascal, the year before either of them first set eyes on the boy Troy. Orion's Night had come round again and Caspar, with two others, was leading his chosen boy down a long, dank passage. The youth, blindfolded and bound, had been told he was no more than a sacrificial animal as far as his captors were concerned.

The boy had persuaded himself this was hyperbole, intended only to heighten his master's enjoyment. Because the use of his eyes had been denied him, he could tell when they had left the main part of the mansion only because of the change from hot air to cold and the hollow ringing quality of the voices of the Superiors.

The shift he had been made to wear felt damp around him and the ropes that secured his hands bit into his flesh. His teeth chattered – whether from cold or fear, he did not know. Gooseflesh covered his slim body; the hairs on his arms and legs stood to attention under the garment. His cock was engorged with the anticipation of what he had been told he was about to experience.

The party were soon in the open air, which, thankfully, was warmer than that of the underground tunnel. (Orion's Night fell in late autumn in that part of the land.) Caspar stopped and turned to the three others. The two who guided the boy pushed him down to the ground making him lie flat on his stomach with his face buried in the dewy grass. Caspar smiled slowly at his two priests. Dawn was breaking over Tarne and the red-gold of the sun's rays gave their faces an unreal colour.

Caspar began to decorate his robes with his chains of office and a mantle embroidered with pentagons and strange hieroglyphics. He pulled the oversized hood up over his windswept black hair. Next he shook his baggy sleeves to his elbows allowing freedom to his wrists, before undoing the top three buttons which held the cloth at his throat. The dark wiry hair of his chest sprang forward. The robes were cumbersome garments for the work they had to do that night.

His two officers, both wearing simpler versions of this garb, pulled their hoods over their heads and clasped their hands in front of them, waiting.

Caspar slowly approached both and sprinkled them with some scented oil. This done, his next task was to prepare the flat piece of stone he had brought them to.

He kindled a fire in front of it. When it was burning brightly, he threw a handful of incense on to the flames. The sour smell pervaded the air and hung about them in a low,

3

acrid cloud. He indicated which of the two was to approach first. Before obeying, Leon glanced briefly at Morgan, who returned the look with undisguised jealousy.

This was Leon's first year at Tarne. He had been told what preliminary offices were required of him. He took the bowl which Caspar handed to him and filled it with water from a stream. Up here on the hilltop, there was little more than a trickle running over the rocks but, nevertheless, it was the water of the River Tarne. He took the bowl over to the stone table and emptied it across the surface. The water gathered in puddles where the altar was indented. Leon used his hands to wash the cold rock, cleansing it for the offering they were about to make.

Morgan, now about to take part for the fourth time and impatient to get into the ritual, was then summoned to tie ropes to four iron rings. These rusting hoops had been driven into the altar by Caspar's great-grandfather, Tarne, the man who had given the village his name.

A cloud passed over the rising sun and a cool breeze swept round the group. Caspar smiled. He liked it when nature added her special effects to this annual drama.

The boy was trembling from head to foot. Caspar placed his foot on the small of his prisoner's back. The boy tried to contain himself but he could not. Caspar put more pressure behind his foot. Still the captive trembled. He raised his blindfolded eyes and let out an unsteady hiss of air from his open mouth. Caspar abandoned him and joined the others at the table.

'It is nearly time,' he said. 'Are we prepared?'

Morgan and Leon both bowed as he had taught them. They stood apart at the foot of the alter, Caspar between them.

The slave was hoisted to his feet. He was made to raise his bound hands high above his head. Caspar took a knife from his

4

belt and slit the boy's robe from the neck to the hem. It blew open in the wind showing a smooth, naked body which was oiled and glistening in the red light. Leon undid his bonds and Morgan finished the act by stripping him completely. The metal band which was fixed around his upper arm to tell the world that he was not a man but the property of Tarne was the only thing that covered the naked flesh of his body. His torn garment was thrown on to the fire where it blazed briefly before becoming so much ash.

Each took hold of one of his arms and manhandled him to the altar. He was laid upon it and roped face upward, his arms and legs wide. His cock jutted out from his groin: separate from him – obscenely demanding. He was still blindfolded and he still trembled.

'Are you prepared to give yourself?' Caspar asked.

'Yes, master.'

The slave's voice was deeper than might have been expected from the look of him. In fact he was nearly twenty-one, but it wasn't his age that made him suitable as a sacrifice. Caspar claimed he chose them intuitively but Morgan had once dared to suggest it was no more than a random selection from the slaves whose good looks most attracted Caspar. Why else were the Superiors always dark-haired and hirsute, as was Caspar himself, and the slaves fair and smooth-skinned?

The slave tested his bonds. He was tied fast: there was no chance of escape, even if he wanted to try it, and, even now, he wasn't sure that he did. He had not long since been an ordinary young man with his studies newly completed and his parents expecting the announcement of an attachment to some young female. Family, wife, children, work . . . That's what he had been led to believe life was all about. Until he met Caspar.

He had been proud when Caspar had told him how special he was. He had eagerly tried to please his new masters and be worthy of whatever 'honour' was in store. It would have been useless to try to run away. Tarne was miles from anywhere, surrounded by wild moorlands on one side and the sea on the other. It was said those who tried to escape were always brought back, no matter how far they tried to run.

Their chanting completed, the three disrobed. True to tradition (if indeed it was tradition that dictated it), these Superiors were all physically of a type, though Morgan sometimes liked to shave his chest. Even now he had less covering it than the others: the growth was only just above the stubble it had been a week earlier. His groin and his legs showed what would have adorned his body had it been so allowed: thick, black hair surrounded his blunt stub of sex and coursed down his powerful legs.

Leon was more refined. He was an athlete: his muscular frame had been created from the thin, lithe teenager he had once been. He was vain and thought Morgan too crude to be a Superior. He had eastern blood and so was swarthy, exotic. He had taken to wearing an earring, which accentuated the romantic image he had of himself. Even his walk was jaunty and self-aware. His cock was long and slender. It was beautiful, not a brutal tool like Morgan's, but a thing for his own pleasure – an instrument of eroticism. His chest was broad and defined, the smooth down that covered it looked like the brush strokes of an artist, there to add shade to the hollows the muscle created.

Caspar was somewhere in between these two. Like theirs, his hair was jet-black, but his skin was pale, almost white. He had thin red rims under eyes that were of a piercing blue. His brows were too thick, making it seem as though he scowled even when the rest of his face was quite open. His hair was long and black, longer even than that of his two companions, who wore theirs down to their shoulders. It was slightly curled and fell over his forehead, further darkening his face.

In the great hall at Tarne, there was a portrait of his great-grandfather. The two were exactly alike. It might have been supposed the line would be handed down from father to son, but this community had been built on worship of the male body and fatherhood was not compatible with it. It was Caspar's uncle who had trained him. In this manner, the leadership was handed down: from uncle to nephew. Caspar's brother, like their father before him, had sworn no son of his would ever go near the place. The time would come, Caspar was sure. His nephew was still a child, but always there was one in the family with those familiar looks and a taste for beautiful men. It was their tradition and Caspar sought to be a faithful custodian of his birthright.

He climbed on top of the slave and knelt astride him, just below the boy's chin. He fondled his own cock. It was flaccid because of the cold and he needed it to be hard. He placed it on the edge of the slave's lips and, with it, traced the outline of the boy's mouth.

'My organ needs to be brought to life,' he said. 'Use your mouth to make it stiff enough to pierce into your fuck-hole.'

The boy opened his lips and accepted the soft penis into his mouth. He sucked on it furiously but that didn't seem to work. He had the sense to change to a more delicate licking round the purple head and was grateful to feel the penis lengthen inside his throat. He pushed the top of his tongue into the slit and jabbed at it carefully and tenderly. Caspar breathed deeper and the slave was aware of his master's hand encouraging the cock to reach its fully erect state.

It grew like an animal waking from sleep. First, though longer than before, it seemed to stay soft. Then, as it was pushed deep towards his gullet, it became completely hard. The slave gagged on it. He quickly learnt to suck it up and down, feeling the uneven surface of the skin where veins stood out, licking round the head, which was already oozing fluid. He sucked and sucked. It was abruptly taken from him and he was rewarded for his efforts by a slap. His cheek stung and tingled and he tried to find comfort by laying the side of his face against the cold stone.

'You were enjoying that too much. I think it's time we gave you something a little more taxing.'

He didn't know what it was they put into his arsehole but it was bigger than a cock and wider. It was slippery with grease, but it was ridged and, even when the first wide part had been accommodated inside him, he knew he must suffer the same pain again as the next part was forced in. He panted, and sweat began to trickle down his body. The thing was gradually swallowed by his gut.

'Soon, that cock which you have just made hard with your mouth, will be inside you where this phallus is now.'

Caspar pushed it one last time and twisted. The slave felt it nudge at his prostate gland and the pain was superseded by an aching warmth which made his heart thump and his stomach turn over inside him. He tried to pull his legs even further apart, tried to push his body further down to allow even more of the obstruction to fill him. However, it was fully implanted and his efforts only resulted in his pulling on his arms causing the metal which encircled his wrists to graze his skin.

One of the other two – he guessed it was Morgan – had taken Caspar's place in his mouth. This new cock was already erect. He caressed it with his tongue and sucked on it urgently. His neck was aching from the unnatural position he was forced to take in order to give satisfaction. He didn't care any more. His fears had gone; he was to be used for sex in the way he most desired to be. He was longing for these three bodies and was grateful he had been chosen to be used by them.

Caspar had encased his tool in a rubber sheath. He ran his hand over it, feeling the smooth, thin covering clinging to the sensitive skin of his penis. He knelt over his victim's knees and, before entering, he spent some time pushing and twisting the phallus in the young boy's anus. Each movement made the slave squirm more. By the time Morgan withdrew from his mouth, the lad was almost in a frenzy of desire.

Caspar lay full length over him and tasted his lips, which still had the salt of Morgan's pre-come on them. He pushed his tongue into the waiting mouth and kissed him violently. Then he rose and indicated Leon should have next use of his face.

Leon sat on the slave, pushing his anus against the hot, wet lips. He moved this way and that, dictating, by the way he shifted his body against the eager tongue, where the boy should lick. He came to rest where he could be pleasured right inside his arse. The slave responded with relish to the unspoken command. His tongue flicked against the knot of muscle and then pushed inside. He was able to get his tongue well up Leon's anal passage. It lapped in and out, going a little further up him each time. Leon, meanwhile, took the lad's nipples in between his fingers and pinched them hard. The slave was sensitive there and the pain spurred him on to more furious arse-licking.

Then it was time for Caspar to fuck his sacrifice. He placed a log under the small of the boy's back, raising the target to where all could see it. The phallus was still inside, stretching the hole painfully. Caspar removed it in one agonising pull, quickly replacing it with his, now enormous, prick. He lay on top of his prisoner as he had before, but this time he didn't kiss him.

He fucked him roughly and brutally, taking no account of the boy's pleasure. The other two stood close to the sides of the table and wanked themselves over the captive body and the man who invaded it.

The three came almost together: Caspar orgasmed inside the slave's arse, groaning and spluttering. He knelt upright to let the last drops of semen seep from his cock. Leon and Morgan narrowly missed hitting him with their spunk, which instead splashed in great white puddles across the slave's chest.

The boy hoped this signalled the point where he would be given his own sexual release. His cock had hardly been touched save by the contact it had had with Caspar's body.

He lay there with the come drying on him. Even the fact that his hands and feet were chained added to his desire to come. The sweet irony of their preventing him from doing so of his own accord did nothing but further increase his desire. He pulled again at his bonds. They yielded not at all. He considered asking them to put the phallus back inside him. He wisely decided it was not his place to talk in any way, certainly not to ask for physical favours.

All three had grouped around him and their hands stroked his naked body. His cock was not touched.

'You will not be going back to Tarne,' Caspar said quietly. 'You are spent now and there is no use for you there.'

'What's to be done with him?' Morgan asked.

'He's worth good money. Sell him to the Illyrians – he should fetch a decent price at the slave market. Unless . . .'

The slave felt the tip of a knife touch his throat and, without being able to help himself, he screamed. Leon raised his voice to protest but Caspar stopped and tossed the knife on to the ground.

'No, do as I tell you. Morgan, take him to the harbour and find a slave-trader. They should be willing enough to take him: they usually have to content themselves with vagrants and criminals.'

The boy was released briefly from his bonds. He was made to kneel and put his hands behind him so they could be bound. He dared not protest but he trembled violently. He had heard dreadful stories of Illyria: how slaves were savagely whipped as a matter of routine, how they were sometimes chained to posts in the street to be used by any passer-by who might take a fancy to them, how their status was less than that of an animal.

Morgan roped him around the chest, pinning his arms to his sides. He was to remain naked from now on. He was taken away, a piece of property now, perhaps regretting ever having succumbed to his own masochistic desires.

Caspar looked across at Leon, who had said nothing, but was still able to convey his disapproval.

'It's important that they don't come back to Tarne,' Caspar said. 'I realise that now. If anything, I've been too soft with him.'

'Do you really believe everything your ancestor wrote in his journal?' Leon asked.

'Yes,' Caspar replied. 'At first I didn't think it was true. But now . . . My great-grandfather found the secret of being young and virile for ever. I will do it.'

'He didn't find anything. Murdering innocent young men didn't save him from the plague. He was dead by the time he was thirty.'

Caspar might not have heard any of this. He picked up the knife and ran his finger over the blade. A line of blood oozed out on to his skin and he smiled.

'I will do it,' he repeated. 'Next year. Just you see.'

Pascal

A year later

The sun was streaming in through the glass above the door, but otherwise the rooms were curtained against the daylight. I thought this was strange, but Caspar had seemed a rather odd sort of person when we first met. I didn't think anything of it: I presumed he had stayed up all night and slept for most of the day. I didn't comment on his appearance or ask what he'd been doing. He wasn't the sort to invite such intrusive pleasantries.

'It's Pascal. We met at the party. I just thought I'd see how you are,' I said.

I felt as though I was intruding. He didn't look well, although his pallor was rather fetching against the darkness of his hair. His eyes, though pink-rimmed through lack of sleep, were still twinkling blue and I was drawn, as before, to the mat of black hair poking over the top of his jerkin. Though he was thinner than I remembered him from our first meeting, three weeks prior to my visit, he still looked like he carried lots of lean, toned muscle.

'The timing of your visit is significant. I'm glad you're here,' he said. Then he stepped aside to allow me into the house.

I seemed to remember he lived alone. Whatever he'd actually told me, it left me confident he had no partner. I wasn't sure whether I could fill this gap in his life but I was determined to find out. The first hurdle over, I said a silent prayer of thanks to gods I didn't believe in and stepped inside.

I knew his income came from his family and I had supposed he'd inherited a great deal of money. I was surprised, therefore, to find the room into which I was ushered comfortable, but Spartan.

He was looking at me in a curious way, as if working out for himself what the real reason for my call might be. It was obvious I had not, as claimed, 'dropped by'. Caspar's house was miles from the village where I had grown up and still lived.

On our first meeting, we had joked about the guests who had all too quickly got down to the business of turning the polite drinks party into an orgy. At first, I had presumed him to be one of the few people around the area whose predilections drew them to women. He certainly hadn't seemed interested in the naked male flesh which quickly filled the rooms of our host. He had claimed, not very convincingly, he was against such indulgence. He followed some religion (I presumed it to be such, though he had described it merely as a 'method for living'). They were some few weeks away from a special day in their calendar and, from what I gathered, he was abstaining from physical pleasure in deference to it. 'The Night of Orion' he called it. He hadn't explained further and I had no idea when it fell.

Later, I had asked him about sex. He'd told me he enjoyed it and then just smiled. I'd given up all hope of bedding him and turned my energies over to conversation and friendship.

The truth was I liked him very much. Not just his looks,

13

which were lovely, but his quiet assurance and his ability to put me at my ease. There was something more about him which I couldn't quite define. Perhaps it was a danger – a hidden violence. He hid much of his thoughts behind a casual veneer which stirred my emotions and lent him a thrilling magnetism.

It was different today. I felt I was meeting a different side of him. He must have known I found him desirable and yet he acted as though he took my excuse at face value and assumed I had called for a chat. Even so, I knew he was pretending and he knew I knew it.

'Come into the main room,' he told me. 'There's a fire in the grate. We might as well be warm.'

There are many houses such as this one dotted about the moorlands surrounding my village. They were once the dwellings of slave-traders who made their livings by selling captives to an island, Illyria, some six miles out to sea. Illyria was once populated entirely by men who indulged themselves from morning till night. Their slaves were the unfortunate people who had been captured in war or simply stolen away from their homes. Stories of the markets where men were sold to other men had been popular in the taverns at home. Although there was a given disapproval of what had gone on, the interest was always evident among the locals.

I had often dreamt of going there to see what it was like today. I had, on more than one occasion, fallen asleep, letting my subconscious mind act out my own capture. I had seen myself taken from my home in chains and, linked to others like me, marched to the waiting slave ship. I always awoke before the point where I was stripped and prepared for selling. Sometimes I found a damp patch on the sheets where my cock had let go its juices.

My first impressions proved to hold true throughout the house. Caspar had almost nothing in the way of decoration or home comforts. There were two piles of cushions on which to

14

sit and a long wooden table. Pewter mugs were set ready and a jug of wine was waiting.

'You're expecting someone else,' I began. 'If you'd rather I went . . .'

He looked me straight in the eye and smiled. Evidently his other guest could wait. He said nothing. I shifted from foot to foot. I was aware of a growing bulge, pushing out the thin material of my trousers.

Although I held out little hope of being physical with Caspar, I had taken care to exercise that morning. I have a good body. It isn't exactly rippling with muscle, but I'm neither overweight nor am I too thin. I have a decent pair of biceps and well-defined pectorals. My legs are sturdy and dusted with a fine covering of appealing hair. I am smooth elsewhere and, although my hair is fine, it is silky and of a pleasant mid-brown colour. I hoped all this would be appreciated and, somehow, I felt it was.

The silence had gone on for longer than was normal. Although Caspar seemed unabashed, I was compelled to say something to make things appear to be more relaxed.

'How have you been?' I asked. It was a fatuous question, the sort of thing you would ask of your maiden aunt. He just gave a slight smile and went over to poke the fire.

'Are you cold?' he said at long last.

I shook my head. Then I realised I was still wearing my cloak. I gave a pathetic little laugh and shrugged it from my shoulders. He took it and placed it carefully on a hook. His eyes appraised my body. There was electricity in the air. I knew something was going to happen. I decided to stop pretending polite indifference and to let him do things in his way.

He must have noticed my relaxation. 'That's better,' he said. 'There's no need to pretend with me. I think we both know what this is all about. Don't we?' This last was added with full meaning. I nodded and gulped. For some reason I was trembling.

'Strip naked.'

The command was so unexpected I wondered if I hadn't imagined it. I felt my heart quicken. I had been right!

Soon my clothes were in a dishevelled mess on the floor at my feet. Caspar had simply watched without assisting, without moving. Now he moved closer to me and stroked his hand down the front of my chest. I drew in breath sharply.

'You like that, do you?' he said. His voice was quiet and sure.

'Yes,' I confessed.

He gave me a corrective slap across the face. Not hard, but hard enough. His body was touching mine. He looked me straight in the eye.

'Yes, what?'

'Yes, sir,' I corrected myself. How he realised this was what I wanted I didn't know. It was more than I could have hoped for from him. With all my night-time fantasies, I had never once been able to experience more than a reluctant charade of domination.

Behind my all too evident desire there was a frisson of fear. For all I knew, the slave trade might still exist in Illyria. Caspar might, after all, be one of those exotic people for whom houses like this had originally been built. In a few hours I might be experiencing what I had always dreamt about. I could find myself in chains, aboard a slave ship, one of many men being transported to spend our lives as the chattels of other men.

'I'm going to hurt you, you know that.'

I nodded again. My cock was rigid. I couldn't deny it was what I wanted.

'Good.' He disappeared for a few moments, returning with a few coils of rope and some strips of material.

'Now,' he said in a practical way. 'I'm going to tie you to the table. I shall tie your hands, but not your legs. I enjoy it

16

when my boys try to defend themselves. Of course you'll be able to kick all you want, but it will do you not the slightest bit of good. That's how I like it. Lie face downward on the table please.'

I did so. He took my wrists and deftly bound each to a leg of the table. He pushed a cushion under my groin, forcing my arse upward to make it more vulnerable as a target. I could indeed move my legs, but only as far as the back of my knees. He seemed pleased that I'd tried.

'You see, you're quite helpless. I shall have you gagged this first time. You might distract me if you plead for me to stop. And blindfolded, I think. Yes.'

Suiting action to word, he stuffed some of the material in my mouth and then secured it in place with another strip. This done, he made a blindfold out of the rest of it and tied it tightly round my eyes.

I felt strangely comfortable – natural even. This was about as degrading a position as I'd ever experienced. I was in his power completely, yet I trusted him.

'I'm going to beat you of course,' he was saying. 'I shall start by using my hands and then go on to my belt. After I've made your arse nice and red, I shall decide whether or not I want to fuck it. I might, but I also might leave you where you are to think about things for a while. If you're good and take whatever I give you without too much moaning, I may let you come, but that's for me to decide when it's time. Do you understand?'

I nodded as well as I could. The table was hard against my chin and I wasn't able to move my head very much. I contented myself with laying my cheek against the unyielding wood and waiting for what might transpire.

He must have been standing there for some time, looking at me. It seemed like about a quarter of an hour but in fact it was probably only a few minutes. I was conscious of an involuntary movement of my hips. I was just able to rub my cock against the cushion. A light tap on my buttocks warned me to stop.

'I'll decide when you can pleasure yourself. You will stay still until you are given permission.'

As far as I knew, he was still clothed. His hand began to caress my back, very lightly. My skin responded to his touch wonderfully. I was puzzled at his loving touch, but I sensed it was merely a preliminary to the pain that was to come. The stroking became more definite, then hard. Soon he was pressing against the muscles of my back, pushing into them with his knuckles.

Just as I was settling into the rhythm of this, he stopped. The light, careful strokes began again, this time on my inner thighs. He went just as far as my balls but didn't touch them. Then he gave the same treatment to my buttocks.

I tried to stay still, but it was difficult. I wanted to respond physically to his touch. I wanted to touch him in the same way – to share lovemaking. This, however, was going to be different from the sex I had so often had with others. I was not permitted to be an active part of it.

I thrilled again at the image of myself – and of him – which flashed across my mind. I kept telling myself I was tied, gagged and blindfolded. This man was in charge of my fate. I was to be sacrificed to his will.

The first slap was not painful. It came in the middle of the stroking: sharp and definite, but not hard. My arse was sensitised by his touch and I responded by giving a low, lustful moan. Another blow soon followed: this time it was harder and caused me a pleasurable sting. I raised his target area slightly to make it easier for him to strike me and also to show my acquiescence.

'Good boy,' he murmured.

Several slaps followed, each meant to hurt and each effective. I took them without protest of any kind. I think I moaned through the gag, but only for the pleasure of it. I reminded myself I was still bound by pulling at the rope around my wrists and testing its strength. I was secure.

Caspar sat astride my upper thighs. He was indeed still clothed. I could feel the smoothness of his trousers against my skin. He leant over my back and put his palms against my face. I wanted so much to lick his hands, to kiss them. He felt the contours of my face, pressing and pushing like a sculptor might his clay.

'I'm interested,' he said at length. 'Is this what you came round for? Just nod if the answer is "Yes".'

I responded. He patted my shoulder.

'Yes, I thought so. I thought you wanted this when we first met, but I wasn't sure. Your attention seemed to be divided between myself and the young boy: Troy. You remember him?'

I tried to nod again. I wanted him to save the conversation till later. It was distracting.

'Don't worry. I'm going to continue your punishment in a moment or two. It isn't finished yet. Troy, yes. He was a fine figure. You like that sort, do you?'

He continued to talk in this matter-of-fact tone for some time. Troy was beautiful, he said. Apparently, I had assumed he wasn't interested in me and, as the alcohol had affected me (I didn't remember this), I had become maudlin and confessed my supposed love to Caspar. Troy had not joined in the sexual activity. He had sat on the edges of the party, clutching his drink and looking scared. Perhaps he was one for the ladies, Caspar suggested.

'Think of him now as I beat you,' he went on. 'Imagine that youthful body naked and bound next to you. Whatever you suffer will shortly be given to him. That lovely brown hair is tied back so we can see his face more clearly. He's gagged like you are and his sun-browned skin is inviting my belt to redden it. I like smooth boys. Troy is like you, hairless where he should be. I'd like to have the two of you. I'd like –'

His belt came down across me. It was like a cut ripping across my skin. Although I had promised myself not to, I gave a muffled shout of pain. The sting had not died before it was followed by another.

'This is my thicker belt,' he explained. 'I have a thinner one which causes even more pain. I shall use that in a moment or two. For now, just get used to this.'

Yet another blow. I gritted my teeth and tried to be good. I wanted him to be pleased with me. I wanted him to praise the way I took my punishment. I wanted above all for him to beat me as much as he liked and then to fuck me up my arse. I felt sure he would, but if I protested too much he might decide I wasn't worthy of it.

'Six times,' he warned me.

The leather swished through the air and met my tender skin. He counted each swipe. By the fifth I felt tears springing into my blind eyes. The last crack sang in the air like the high note of a stringed instrument. My arse was hot with the effect of it. The hurt subsided and gave way to a warm glow which burned across me. Though I had been in pain, I desired more of the same. I pushed my arse upward to indicate this. He stroked it gently and gave it a pat.

'You're well worth the effort,' he said. 'I'm pleased with you. It's time to give you a little reward.'

He stood and came round to the front of me. I heard him undoing his trousers and pulling them down. Hot, musty-smelling flesh touched my skin. He wiped pre-come across my forehead and rolled his penis against my face.

He undid the gag and pushed his semi-hard member into my eager mouth. I took it and happily began to coax it into full rigidity. It didn't take long. Soon I was sucking and licking that beautiful piece of meat. My nose was deep into the sweat-covered hair of his groin. I choked slightly as his cock hit the back of my throat, but I didn't let up on the job I had been given to do.

20

He pulled away eventually. I heard him gather his clothes back around him.

'Now let's see how you like the other belt,' he said.

He didn't give me any time to prepare myself. The thing cracked at my flesh like a whip. It was far more painful than the first implement. He didn't vary the strokes this time. He gave me ten. By the end of it I was shouting my hurt and pleading with him.

'Please, sir. Please stop. I can't take any more. I'll do anything.'

'You will do anything,' he answered. 'But not as a trade-in for less pain. You'll do anything because I tell you to. I think ten strokes is enough for now. But in future you'll learn to take whatever is given without protest. I don't want to have to gag you each time. Do you understand?'

'Yes, sir,' I whimpered, already despising my weakness. 'I'm sorry, sir.'

'Because of that, I don't think I'll let you come for a while. It won't do you any harm to have to wait. Let me see how tight your pretty little arse is.'

He inserted his forefinger into my hole. It went in easily enough and didn't cause me any discomfort. He pushed another finger in and still I was able to take it comfortably. He withdrew.

'We need something a bit bigger, don't we?'

He found something, I couldn't of course, see what it was. It was cold and had been greased. I thought it was made of some sort of metal. It was tapered and so went in without difficulty. Its girth increased towards its base. As he pushed it further it became more and more difficult to take. I breathed heavily and slowly, trying for all I was worth to keep my vocal cords under control. The end of the metal penis was bulbous: I presumed this was to stop it slipping out easily. It felt like my sphincter was being pulled apart.

Once it was in, I quickly grew used to it. Caspar twisted it and pushed it this way and that. It was now warmed by the heat of my body and it felt good.

'I have decided I will fuck you,' he said. 'This is just to make sure you're ready for me.'

Leaving the thing inside me, he proceeded to undress completely. I heard him moving about the room. I supposed he was putting his clothes in their proper place. He briefly wiped his cock against my lips again – it was now encased in a rubber sheath. Then he squatted so his face was next to mine.

'One kiss,' he told me.

He put his lips against my own and I responded readily. I waited for his tongue to enter my mouth before I dared do as much for him. It was a passionate exchange and one I would remember for some time. I felt I wanted to surrender completely to this man in every way. I wanted to tell him to debase me by every means he thought fit. I wanted to be his in every conceivable part. My emotions had been conquered utterly.

When he had had enough he climbed on top of me and, as he had before, leant over my back, his torso close against my skin. I felt the hairs on his chest tickle and prick; I felt the warmth of his body; I smelt his sweat and the cleaner, more delicate odour of his washed head hair. He had the belt in his hands. Removing the dildo in one, clean pull, he placed the belt in between my teeth.

I bit into the leather and prepared to be invaded by his flesh.

Holding the belt tight, riding me in every sense of the word, he jabbed his hard penis against my pleasantly sore arse. It slipped into me straightaway. He was able to give me his full length virtually in one movement. I was filled by his meat.

He fucked me slowly, bucking up and down. As he did this, he gave me regular whacks across the sides of my buttocks with his free hand. His other hand pulled on the belt, stretching my neck and forcing my head upward.

The rhythm of his movement increased in pace. He was

more urgent now. I sensed he was close to coming. As he approached his climax, he began to pant. His cock rammed home two, three, four times: disjointed, frantic stabs. He sighed deeply and stopped.

I didn't want him to pull out of me. But he did – and I felt suddenly deprived. I felt he had become one with my body and I was now missing something that was as vital to me as one of my limbs.

He undid the blindfold and kissed me again. I drank thirstily from his lips, sucking his spittle into my mouth and pushing my tongue against his. He allowed this for some minutes before pulling away and undoing my hands.

'Right,' he said. His voice was still very normal: he might just as well have been suggesting dessert after a good meal. 'I want to see you wank yourself off. Stand up.'

I obeyed. My legs were stiff and I stumbled slightly. He told me to masturbate myself slowly. He told me he was just going to watch me do it. He sat back on the cushions and I positioned myself in front of him. This in itself was humiliating. I had never wanked in front of someone who wasn't taking any part in it. Here I was, abusing my body, not to give myself pleasure, but for him to see.

I stroked my throbbing penis, trying to go slowly as he had told me. Every time the strokes got faster, he gestured for me to hold back.

When I came it was because I simply had to. I usually rub frantically at my prick before orgasm, the increased friction aiding the intensity of the spurt from my balls. This time it arrived unbidden, coming shooting out like a fountain. I didn't know I was capable of producing so much. The concentrated thrill that had produced it stayed with me for some seconds after I had spent every bit of fluid. Caspar smiled.

'You wanted that, didn't you?'

'Yes. Yes, sir,' I agreed.

'You can stop the "sir" now,' he told me. 'Get dressed if you want to. I think I'm going to stay naked for a while.'

'Then I will too,' I said.

I lay down on the cushions next to him and stroked his chest hair lovingly. I wanted to tell him how much it had all meant to me, but words seemed inappropriate. I somehow realised it was not the right time to voice my feelings.

We lay there for ten minutes or so. He allowed me to caress his body and even to kiss his cheek. I tried to reach his lips, but he turned his face away. I laid my head against his pectoral muscles and kissed his smooth, brown nipple. I dared to nibble it gently. He let me do this for a while but then rose and busied himself with tidying the room.

'I won't be your lover I'm afraid,' he said. 'I'd like to take your body when it suits us both. Maybe I'll have you chained to my bed one night. That's what you want and that's what I'm prepared to give. If you need more, you'll have to ask your other man.'

'I don't have another man,' I said. 'I want you.'

'No, you don't. I'm just the first one who's given you the sex you need. There will be others. Anyway, you do have another man. What about this Troy we talked about?'

There was something in the way he said this that caused me to be suspicious. Underneath his casual way, I knew he was planning something. I had no reason to suppose he was doing anything more than playing secret matchmaker to the two of us, but I recognised in myself an instinctive jolt of fear. A childhood story flashed across my mind: a wicked magician showing some poor, innocent youth a cave of treasure. I didn't remember what happened, but I recalled declaring at the time I would never fall for such an obvious trick.

'He's not interested in me,' I said.

'You don't know that. We'll have to find a way of getting him where you want him.'

He paused for a moment, thinking. Then he went on: 'Tell

24

me, do you want him to dominate you like I just have? Or would you like to see him bound and gagged? I believe absolutely you could have either, or both.'

'I don't know,' I replied.

This was a lie. I did know. I wanted Troy to be subservient. His youthful frame and his smooth good looks were not conducive to being master. I wondered why I couldn't discuss my lustful feelings in the same easy way that Caspar seemed to employ so readily. Perhaps I was ashamed of them; perhaps I was still thinking of the magician and his tempting treasure; or perhaps I wanted Caspar to see me as a complete slave. To admit to desires that matched his own might put him off the notion (which I still hoped he held) that we were compatible. He seemed to be able to read my thoughts.

'I will have you again, you needn't worry about that. It doesn't matter to me if you like to have others in whatever way you choose. I'll enjoy teaching you how you should treat a slave. Come over here.'

I stood beside him and he put his arm around me. He was a curious mixture of sadistic lust and loving romance. The fact that I knew him to be capable of switching from a caress to a blow made me all the more desirous of his attention. There was danger in his kisses and his gentle touch could, as I had just learnt, be a prelude to the pain of a beating.

He was looking at a picture on the wall. It was of a little village which nestled in between green hills. The sea was just visible in the far distance. It had been painted by an inexpert hand, but it was a pleasant enough ornament.

'Where is it?' I asked.

'Tarne. It's a secret place: cut off from everywhere. Last night was a special festival there – the night for Orion's children. It already seems so long ago.'

'It looks very nice,' I said lamely.

Orion's children? This then explained his pallid appearance. I had blundered in the very morning after his ceremony.

25

'You'd like it there. Perhaps I should take you,' he said.

Maybe this was his way of showing he wanted our relationship to be more than just sex. Maybe he wanted a romantic weekend in this picturesque little place. I agreed to the proposal enthusiastically.

'Yes,' he continued. 'You'd fit in there very well. There's a large house which is owned by a community of men. I may have mentioned: I have an interest in it. I'd like very much for you to meet them. Perhaps . . .' He paused to give his words more significance. 'Perhaps you could bring Troy.'

I protested I didn't know the boy. I had hardly spoken to him. I had no idea where he lived. I didn't know if he was involved with someone. All these objections were disregarded.

'He couldn't possibly object to an invitation. You can ask whoever it was that gave the party where you can get in touch with him. If he has a lover, then he'll say no and we'll be no worse off. I think it would be a good idea.'

My cock was rising again. I think it was because of his having his arm around me. I ventured to mirror his action but he pulled away from my embrace. My erection had not gone unnoticed.

'Again?' he asked. 'I wouldn't have thought you'd be capable of more. It will take me a while to get all the spunk out of the carpet.'

I smiled weakly and stroked my cock. His was still limp, but I saw it twitch promisingly.

'No,' he said firmly. 'I won't allow it just yet. Come with me.'

He went into another room and I followed. It was much like the room we had just vacated but there were manacles on the walls. Most were about shoulder height. On seeing them my erotic thoughts became like a whirlwind in my head. My hopes were realised soon enough.

He told me to stand against the wall and to raise my arms. When I had done this he secured each of my hands into the iron rings. He had brought the gag with him and he soon had it in my mouth.

'I'm going to leave you here for some time, so you might as well get used to it,' he told me. 'When I come back tonight, I'll decide whether you've been good enough to share my bed. If for any reason you haven't, you'll sleep on the floor with your neck chained to the bedpost.'

He pressed his naked body into mine and blew his hot breath into my face. He stood back and took my nipples in between his fingers. He squeezed them and pulled them. I writhed under his touch, desperately hoping he would take my cock. He didn't: he left me alone in the room. The door slammed and a key was turned in the lock.

I tried to make sense of what my emotions were telling me. Was I in love with this enigmatic person? Was it perhaps, as he claimed, just lust? I had lost all sense of dignity or self-respect. I would happily have walked naked behind him in public with a notice around my neck declaring me to be his slave.

A couple of hours passed and my erection subsided. I think I fell asleep, but the discomfort of my position prevented me from going too deeply into slumber. I was aware of the room, aware of my chains. Images of Caspar and the punishment he had just given me floated in and out of my mind. I hoped my arse had been marked by his belts.

I imagined what it would be like to be taken publicly by him. I thought again of Illyria and the slave market. My usual dream of being sold came in snatches: in the crowd that surrounded us captives, Caspar stood. He was the man who I knew would buy me. I would belong to him legally and be made to forfeit any rights I might have in my own body. He would be my master.

Again and again, his face came back to me. I remembered the smell of his hair, the feel of his skin, the warmth of his cock.

'Caspar,' I said out loud. 'Caspar, I want you. Take my body; it belongs to you.'

I kept repeating such useless phrases and found them comforting in a small way. I realised then the point of his making me suffer this prolonged bondage. He was forcing me to consider what had passed between us. He was confirming me as a subservient. This was the most important part of my initiation. I couldn't lie to myself and my chains prevented me from finding other distractions to fill my mind.

I was not in love with him. I was in love with his belt, with his hand across my buttocks, with his rope and his chains.

I was a slave. I had no right to be in love. I was there to be used by whoever wanted me. By whoever owned me.

One

The man paused by the old gate that admitted visitors to the village. A rough wooden sign was all the welcome it proffered: it read TARNE.

He'd been led to believe the place was pleasant: romatic even. It now appeared to be dilapidated and it had a distinct air of brooding. Some old, run-down homesteads lined the one and only street. Off in the distance, on the hill, the gloomy walls of an ancient folly loomed out of the evening mist. He shuddered.

There was no one about. A deathly silence prevailed. He picked up his battered case, pulled his woollen cloak around him and trudged on towards the unwelcoming folly.

Denton was in his early thirties. The journey he had under-taken had been arduous and he was beginning to feel at least ten years older. Being hatless, he was afforded no protection against the wind, which had got up in the last hour of his travelling. (He had a paranoid belief that the bad weather had waited until he had left the protection of the carriage: it had been a fine and warm autumn evening before.) He had had little sleep and so his eyes, he knew, were swollen and the lines in his strikingly intense face were deeper than normal. Even so, his looks warranted the attentions of the women in the city and, had he but known it, not a few of the men. He had dark, copper-coloured hair, sweeping back from a high forehead. His sharp, angular face could have belonged to a painter or a poet, but his body was by no means effeminate or thin. He was proud of his strong arms and legs and was never ashamed of baring his chest at the gymnasium he had attended since his early twenties. He had fine hair on his forearms and legs: dark, reddish-brown hair which tempted his secret admirers to stroke it. He carried himself well and assuredly, safe in the knowledge of the effect he created, but with enough diffidence to prevent conceit. He had been advised to dress down so as not to attract curiosity. As a result he had chosen a jerkin made of cheap cloth which did little to keep out the biting wind. He was glad of his cloak which, though expensive, didn't look it.

How long would he have to stay here? he wondered. He thought of his wife and family far away. They would, no doubt, already be concerned for his safe return, or, to be more accurate, they would be concerned for the safe return of their regular income. Still, as he'd often said, such investigations were his profession. Without these jobs, they wouldn't be able to bleed his wallet as was their wont. Anyway, he had con- sidered carefully beforehand: he'd dealt with all his misgivings. Now was not the time to resurrect them.

He had in his case a portrait of the boy. It had been painted some years before and the lad's parents had been at pains to point out that he might no longer have the same hairstyle; he might have grown a beard; he might have changed his mode of dress. Denton grunted, going over what he had wanted to say in his mind: 'Not much use my having the portrait, then, is it?'

Personally, he thought his errand was going to be a waste of his own time and his employers' money. He had heard about the community of Tarne before. Brainwashing perhaps? Or young people with ridiculous notions in their heads, who, after all, had the right to choose an inadvisable and, it was said, immoral lifestyle. He might well find the lad but, even if he did, what chances were there of persuading him to go back to his parents?

In truth he felt some sympathy for the runaway. The couple he had met were hardly the sort of loving family one might wish to run home to. The old man had far too much money and his arrogance and unpleasantness matched his wealth. The woman was domineering and a hypochondriac. She had twice threatened to faint dead away when the possibility of a negative result had been suggested to her. Still, as Denton often told himself, they were paying him and they were the ones who must call the shots.

In the centre of the village was a shabby tavern. There were signs of life inside. Perhaps this might be the best place to begin his investigations. Although the hostelry was hardly inviting, he welcomed the thought of a drink. He much enjoyed a beer or two, even though he was careful of his diet and alcohol was not something he took every day. He spent enough time exercising each morning: his body was well defined and healthy. He could afford to ignore the irritating 'good angel' which nagged him from behind his left ear.

He was immediately aware of his entrance having an effect on the few people who were sitting drinking in there. The conversation didn't exactly stop, but it sort of slowed down. Nobody looked at him directly, but he could feel their eyes glancing in his direction. They were clearly not used to strangers. Why should they be? No stranger would choose to spend any time in this drear place unless they had to.

The landlord, however, was a cheerful enough fellow. He wiped his hands on a cloth and gave a little jerk of the head in anticipation of his customer's order. Denton asked for a jug of

31

ale and took a place at a table in the corner, away from the other drinkers.

Three of the clientele were older people: older than Denton at any rate. They were working types, possibly farmers. Two of them were deep in conversation; one sat alone, smoking a long clay pipe. The clouds from this hung around him, aromatic and mysterious. The other two were remarkably attractive younger men. Denton never publicly acknowledged any attraction towards his own sex, but he would admit to appreciating the aesthetic quality of a handsome face.

One of these lads was slouching in his chair with his eyes half closed. He may have been drunk. The other sat patiently beside him, looking down at the floor. His attitude was one of servitude. Unlike his companion, who was well covered against the bad weather, he was wearing an open shirt and tight trousers which showed off the power of his legs. Round his neck was a leather collar with a metal loop at the back of it. Denton's keen eyes noticed the leash on the table between them. They were evidently residents of the community he had been sent to look into.

Denton shivered. He had been too long in the constraints of his empty marriage to be able to look on this show without blushing. He would rather not have had to see such unashamed behaviour for it made the path he had chosen in life all the more difficult to defend, even to himself. If men wanted to screw other men, why couldn't they do it out of sight of those who were not able to enjoy another's body? It was bad enough having the temptation of that damned island, but at least the intervening sea kept him out of harm's way. His good angel smiled upon him and, not for the first time, he wished it dead.

The ale was set before him and he paid for it. The landlord hovered by the table, perhaps waiting for a gratuity. Denton gave him another coin and invited him to sit down and share the jug of beer.

Having brought himself a tankard from the bar, the landlord poured out two measures and quaffed a large amount of his own in one go. Denton sipped, wondering how best to get the man to talk.

'Visitors are a bit of an event for us,' the landlord began. Denton resisted the temptation to be sarcastic and explained he was 'just passing through'. He'd lost his way he said. The landlord immediately enquired where he was headed. Denton kicked himself. He might have known that such a lame explanation would provoke this sort of question and he had no ready answer.

'Just travelling, here, there and everywhere,' he said.

The landlord nodded. 'I see,' he said. He meant it.

'I have a son. He needs money,' Denton lied. 'I've put together all I can and I'm trying to find him in order to pass it on. I know he came this way, but I don't know where he ended up. I thought perhaps . . .'

'You don't want to ask me, sir. You should have a word with those two. Or at least with the one who's allowed to talk. His name's Morgan and the other one is Cuthwin. I fear Morgan's not really in a state to be too helpful and his little friend will not say a word without having permission to do so. It's the way they do things, but no doubt you already know that.'

'I see you've found me out,' Denton said, deciding to encourage the conversation. 'Yes, my son is very likely one of the lads who live in the old house up there. I found out where he was, but I meant what I said. I'm not here to cause any trouble. I merely want him to have enough money to see him out of his present difficulties.'

'Why would he need cash?' the landlord asked. 'They might be odd. They might even be weird by your standards and mine, but they look after their own. They have enough money to see to their needs. We don't often get them in here, but we do occasionally. I've never seen any of them who was starving.'

33

The drunken Morgan suddenly came to. He grabbed his companion under the chin and gave him a kiss, full on the lips. Then he laughed and rocked back on his chair. The other responded only as long as contact was made, after which he resumed his passive stance. The two other customers, who sat talking together, watched briefly and then resumed their conversation. They didn't appear to be disconcerted by this behaviour. The solitary man with the pipe belched and watched for further activity.

Morgan leant over and slapped a bag of coins on to the table in front of his servant. Cuthwin rose without a word and moved to the counter. He waited patiently, not looking in the landlord's direction: the innkeeper didn't seem to be in a hurry to serve him.

'He's one of the lower ones,' he explained to Denton. 'They come in two groups – the lower and the higher. The higher ones they call "Superiors". The lower ones enjoy being like the slaves of the old days. They sometimes come in here with all sorts of bruises and marks on their bodies. I can't say it's the sort of thing that makes my cock jump to attention, but . . . each to his own. What do you say?'

'Each to his own,' agreed the other. He raised his tankard in salutation and took a swig of ale. 'Aren't you going to give him a drink?' he asked.

'Like I said, they enjoy being treated like shit. If I jumped up every time one of them came to the bar, it would only confuse them. I'll go over when I'm ready.'

'You'll go over now, you ignorant pig!'

The shout came from the drunken youth. He was swaying visibly and waving his empty tankard at the landlord. 'I want some more beer!' he slurred. 'Now!'

'Yes, sir,' said the innkeeper. He didn't seem to be vexed at the youth's rudeness. 'He's one of the Superiors,' he whispered unnecessarily.

He served the beer. Some of it he poured into a tankard and

this was duly dispatched to Morgan who slurped away without giving any thanks to either party. The other measure he poured into a small wooden bowl which he placed on the floor by the servant's chair. The youngster paid for both and then crouched on all fours and began to lap at the beer like an animal who had been given its milk. Nobody remarked on this. Nobody even took any notice.

The landlord produced another jug for his new friend and himself and rejoined Denton at table.

'I remember going to Illyria when I was just about his age,' he said. 'What a place! Did you ever go when it was in its heyday?'

Denton shook his head. This too was a lie. He had been there many times. His own father had worked on the slave market for some years. When Denton was only eighteen or so, he had found out about sex from one of his father's slaves. The adolescent fumblings had been exciting enough at the time, but, he'd managed to persuade himself, were nothing compared with the experience of having a woman – something he had had to wait another five years for. He had often wondered if his father indulged in 'abnormal' sex. Certainly he never condemned it. His mother had always maintained theirs was a happy marriage, but then she had put up with most of his father's foibles. Maybe men were just another disagreeable thing she had learnt to ignore.

'Since they allowed the women over there, I'm told things aren't the same at all,' the landlord was saying. 'It still goes on as before around the main town, but I remember when the whole island was given over to sodomy. That's why places like the old mansion up there came into existence. They had to go somewhere, didn't they?'

Denton didn't want to get into a conversation in which he might have to reveal his own, hidden desire to touch the beauty of other men's bodies. He remained noncommittal. His job didn't pay so much he found it necessary to lay his vulnerability open to strangers. Evasiveness came easy to him after so many years. Even the landlord's obvious acceptance of his customers' preferences did not encourage him to lower his guard.

'What do the others in the village think about it?' he asked.

'There was some opposition when they all came here, but that was a long time ago. You get used to anything when it's there in front of you all day and every day. Look around you. Do you see those three layabouts objecting?'

Denton had to admit there was no evidence of any offence being caused. His bad angel appeared and began to beckon him towards a door which he'd locked years before. 'What have you got to lose?' it asked. He dismissed it immediately.

'Illyria's still a colourful place to visit,' the landlord said. 'I like a woman in my bed. I do, I don't deny it. On the other hand, when you see some of what goes on ... Well, when I've had too much of this stuff, I don't mind a bit of boy-arse.'

This comment was made more to himself than to Denton. He was watching the two young lads. Cuthwin had finished lapping at his beer and was now sitting back on his haunches waiting for his master to pay him some attention. The other drank away, his face covered by the upturned tankard. His hand, however, soon found its way to his slave's chest and was tweaking at one of his erect nipples. When he had fully contented himself with one, he went on to the other. The boy suffered this indignity without complaint. His face was only slightly contorted with the pain of it.

'Shirt!' Morgan barked out. The slave compliantly removed the offending garment and laid it on the floor. His back was a mass of red welts going this way and that.

'See what I mean?' the innkeeper said. 'He's been under the whip and not too long ago is my guess.'

Denton tried to hide his interest. He remembered his father whipping slaves. He had often been made to watch. The implication was always that he would receive a similar beating if he wasn't a good son and did everything he was told. Needless to say, the warning had been effective: his father had never found it necessary to whip him. The boy who had given him his first orgasm was often told to strip, to kneel, to bend his back and then keep his body still so Denton's father could decorate it with stripes. Denton remembered 'kissing them better'. The slave had often said it was worth the punishment to receive the sympathetic love that would surely follow.

Once, Denton had lost his temper over some unimportant trifle and had taken it out on his slave-lover. He had surprised the lad by ordering him to strip completely naked – something his father never did. He had then lashed him for a full ten minutes, using the five-tailed scourge which was kept for the most outrageous misdemeanours. His lover had taken it without question and had not complained when Denton had given him the added offence of pushing his face into the mud and spitting on him. There had been no apology; there had been no conciliatory lovemaking. Denton had preferred to forget the incident had ever happened.

That good angel had given him some pause, but he had, as always, tried to ignore it. Soon after that time he had left his father's house for good.

He always wondered what had become of the slave. Illyria still permitted men to own others, but the mainland had had a wave of liberal thought sweep over it. Puritanical elders had taken many of the positions of power and many such as Denton had chosen to deny they ever went through a 'phase' of loving, or fucking, other men. The family; procreation; 'decency' . . . These were the things to believe in, the things to promote. Since his marriage he had tried to think of his earlier dalliance as having been an evil thing. His father's slave had tempted him into doing something that was totally against his nature. He had now put all that messy business well into the book of past history. Of course, he didn't believe his own words no matter how often he tried.

37

'I need to fuck you,' the drunken youth announced. He might well have been talking to any of the men in the tavern, but of course the object of his desire knew full well he was not.

'Surely you don't let them do it here?' Denton asked, hoping against hope the landlord did precisely that.

He was colouring obviously and he knew it. He was rescued by a laugh from the innkeeper.

'It wouldn't bother me if they did. No, I don't. They can go upstairs like they usually do. I think our friend might need a hand.' He realised the unintentional double entendre. 'I mean he might need helping up the stairs. His slave has to go up first to make himself ready.'

He had already gone on ahead. The youth who had spoken finished his beer, farted loudly and rose unsteadily to his feet.

'Landlord!' he yelled.

'All right, sir. I'm coming to get you,' the landlord said cheerily. He assisted the young man across the floor and up the stairs. A door was audibly opened and slammed shut.

'He'll probably fall asleep and the poor wretch will be made to drink his beery piss in the middle of the night,' the landlord said when back at the table. 'Those two are regulars here. There are quite a few that I never see, save on the road — in passing as it were. Will you be wanting a room, sir?'

Denton considered. He had planned to find somewhere to stay near to the village, but he wasn't sure he could stand being so close to what he wanted so much but what life had forbidden him. On the other hand, it would probably serve his purpose very well and he had his wife's expensive tastes to think about . . . He didn't need to persuade himself further.

'I'll stay at least till morning. Maybe longer. If you have room for me that is.'

'Like I say, I'm not exactly overrun with customers. You're

very welcome, sir. I'll show you to your room whenever you're ready.'

By the time he was preparing himself for bed, Denton was drunk. He never became so inebriated that he didn't know what he was doing, but alcohol always had one unfortunate effect on him. It gave him an overwhelming desire for sex. Usually his wife would grudgingly suffer his alcoholic ardour. Though he never admitted it, even to himself, she was rarely the one he thought of when his climax eventually arrived. He would close his eyes and remember his father's slave of all that time ago. The fact that he had forbidden himself this desire made the image all the more erotic. As soon as he had come, he would lapse back into the old, familiar feeling of shame and guilt. He would wash himself and, without speaking to his scornful, disagreeable spouse, would get into bed, turn away from her and quickly fall asleep. In the morning he would often be in a miserable temper. She had grown used to this ritual and she could seldom be bothered to attempt to brighten his mood. Perhaps she recognised his gloom as the price she had to pay for her financial independence, or perhaps she simply didn't care.

Denton had removed his clothes and was standing with his legs apart, in front of the roaring fire the landlord had prepared for him. The heat licked upward and caressed his hairy legs, his balls and his cock. He rubbed gently over his belly and on, pressing his fingers into his pubic hair, pushing down to either side of his growing penis. He supposed he would have to satisfy himself with a wank. He stroked his large hand over the length of his member. It felt unusually smooth, sensitive to his touch. He pulled his loose foreskin back and, after spitting on his hand, gently rubbed across the bulbous head, causing the whole thing to stand proud – demanding more.

Then he heard a crack from across the corridor. He recognised the sound at once. It was followed by a muffled cry. The two boys were indulging themselves and they were not more than a few feet away.

A scenario went through Denton's head in a rapid series of pictures. He naked, walking across to their room. They hearing the noise of his footsteps and the door suddenly being opened. The thuggish Morgan standing there, his shirt open, his trousers undone. His midriff would be muscled and hairy, would draw Morgan's eyes and keep them fixed upon it. He wouldn't be able to help himself. Then the boy would pull him into the room where the other lad, Cuthwin, would be tied to the bed, face downward, his arse waiting to be fucked or whipped – whatever his master desired. Denton's hand responded to the pictures in his mind by pumping his cock harder. Soon he was on the very brink of orgasm.

And he stopped.

It wasn't enough. Here he was, in this place where men paraded their sexual needs for all to see. He would never have such an opportunity again. Or, if he did, it would be some time before it happened. The beer had made him reckless. It had taken away all the objections he would otherwise have. His cock needed this – *he* needed it. Why content himself with mere images when he could surely have the real thing – and easily?

Carefully, he opened the door. The sounds of Cuthwin being beaten were clearly audible. A strap of some kind was being used on him. It sounded like his face was either pushed into a pillow or he was gagged in some way. His cries were muffled, although they were loud enough.

Denton crept across the landing towards the other room. His head was spinning and he was nervous, but the possibility of plunging his cock into that young, vulnerable arse was spurring him on.

He knelt down and put his eye to the keyhole. The first thing he saw was the back of – presumably – Morgan. He had a terribly thin waist, but it was not indicative of the rest of his torso. His shoulders were broad and powerful. One of his arms was raised, displaying the thick bush of hair which adorned his armpit. The arm came down with force and Denton caught a fleeting glimpse of a leather taws in the boy's hand. It had evidently found its mark, for the action resulted in a cry from the unseen Cuthwin. Morgan moved out of sight and Denton waited, his vantage point now affording him nothing more than a view of the wall.

There was a grunt from Morgan and a moan from Cuthwin. Did this mean they were fucking? Denton had to find out. Ridiculous though it seemed, he automatically invented some stupid excuse for interrupting them. He had the wrong room. That would do. It would be easy enough to wander in by mistake and then . . . Well, the rest would follow.

He stood and prepared himself with an intake of breath and a count of one to three. He opened the door.

Both young men were completely naked. Morgan spun round as the door opened. His body was magnificent. He had shaved his chest – the very faint stubble that covered it betrayed the fact. His skin seemed barely able to contain the rippling tissue that lay beneath it. There wasn't an ounce of fat on his body: from his neck to his thighs, all was hard, pronounced muscle. His legs were very hairy, as was his abdomen. His sleek, black hair was hanging over his forehead, lank from the sweat that his exertion had produced.

The other boy was unable to see who the intruder was, for he was bound hand and foot. He had been placed across a chair with his firm buttocks available for his master's strap. His legs were slender and smooth and he had unusually small feet. No more of him was visible from where Denton stood.

'I'm sorry I . . .'

The prepared explanation disappeared from Denton's mind. His cock was evidence enough of what he was about. Morgan's face registered surprise and then slow delight.

'What's this?' he said. 'Have we woken you?'

'No, no,' Denton began. 'I just . . .'

'You just thought my slave is public property and you decided to avail yourself of his body. Is that it?'

'I'm in the wrong room.'

The boy's tone was sneering and scornful. It quelled some of Denton's ardour and caused it to be replaced with his usual prudishness. Had he been clothed, he would have stuck to his story and left there and then. However, he wasn't clothed and the scene before him was too much simply to ignore.

Morgan approached him and flicked his cock with his finger. Denton wanted to be outraged, but he wasn't: he was uncontrollably excited.

'The wrong room, eh? I don't think so. I think you knew very well which room you wanted to enter.'

Cuthwin was wriggling about on the chair. Denton realised that he was, in fact, rubbing his penis against the hard wood. Morgan turned and gave him a sound thwack across his arse cheeks.

'You can stop that, boy. I'll tell you when you can give yourself pleasure. I haven't finished with you yet.' He turned back to Denton. 'Perhaps you need a belting as well. It might help you remember which room you should be in.'

Denton hadn't considered this. His fantasy had been to use the slave, not to be used by the master. Morgan stood very close to him and he felt the prickle of the stubble on his chest against his own breast. The boy was slightly taller than he was and his hot, beer-smelling breath blew into Denton's face. Their two cocks brushed together, seeking each other out of their own accord. There was silence for a few seconds.

The provocative tone Morgan had used had left Denton embarrassed and tongue-tied. He was now being physically threatened and, incredibly, he was still aroused. He could have taken a step backwards to escape the deliberate invasion of his body space. He could have protested; he could have walked away. He did none of these things.

Morgan smiled unpleasantly and, slowly, so Denton could see it coming, he collected a mouthful of saliva and spat it directly into the older man's face. It hit him in the eyes, blinding him for a moment.

Still he did nothing to protect himself. He even resisted wiping the spit away. He knew this was as good as acquiescing to the boy's proposal. His chance to do otherwise had come and gone.

'I see,' said Morgan. He patted Denton's cheek in a condescending manner and placed the leather strap to the lips of his willing prey.

'Kiss it nicely. It's going to kiss your arse soon.'

Denton abandoned all dignity and tentatively brushed his lips against the leather. Morgan wasn't satisfied.

'I said kiss it — it isn't the cheek of some old hag. Kiss it!'

Denton pressed his face into the leather and felt an unfamiliar warmth spreading across his insides as he succumbed to his desire for humiliation. Morgan had the strap in both hands and was forcing it against his victim's mouth. All the while, his face retained that sneering, scornful expression. He evidently sensed Denton couldn't help but comply, even though a part of him wished otherwise.

Morgan turned his attention to the prostrate Cuthwin. He undid some of the rope and pushed him roughly off the chair leaving him to struggle in the remaining bonds on the floor. Denton sneaked an appreciative glance at the lithe form. Cuthwin was slim and supple. Not particularly developed, but very attractive. His hands were secured behind his back and his ankles looked red and swollen where the rope bit into them. He was gagged, the material flattening his long, brown hair on each side of his thin face. There was a look of adoration in his dark eyes which never left off gazing at his master.

'We'll have you over the chair, like he was. Get to it!'

Feeling clumsy and awkward, Denton crossed the floor and placed himself across the chair. The position was strange to him. It thrilled him and yet he despised himself for the indignity of it. He placed his hands on the floor in front of him and lowered his head. His heart thumped loudly.

He expected the belt to strike him at any second. Mentally he prepared himself for the pain. He was in too deep now. He had to go through with it. He knew that he was big enough and strong enough to escape but he also knew he would never be able to leave off wondering what he might have missed if he backed out now.

He wasn't beaten at first. He was fucked. His arse, unused to invasion of any kind, was suddenly stabbed by seven inches of hot flesh. As it entered him, it felt the same as when he was desperate for a shit, but the relief of passing something out of his anus was not allowed him. Apart from the smooth lubrication of a sheath, Morgan had not greased him or prepared him in any way. The prick pushed upward and inward making him grind his teeth in agony. Then, briefly, the pain subsided as Morgan drew back. The relief was momentary. Morgan's whole body came crashing against his back, forcing the thing back into his guts.

This slow preamble quickly became a rhythmic thrusting which replaced the extreme discomfort with another feeling. Inside him, Denton experienced a glow, somewhere in between physical desire and emotion, which brought him close to tears. Without being bidden and without being able to help it, he groaned:

'Fuck me! Please! Yes, fuck my arse. It feels so good. Put your great cock into me! Yes, fuck me!'

Cuthwin had somehow managed to crawl to a position in front of him. He had struggled on to his knees so his face was near to Denton's. The older main availed himself of it readily. He licked and kissed, all his dignity discarded. Cuthwin was completely passive, just presenting his smooth face to the other and not responding to the frantic contact. His eyes were closed now. Denton looked down at his slender cock which jutted out from a nest of fair pubic hair. He wanted to take that cock into his mouth and suck on it like a baby comforting itself with his father's thumb.

Morgan pulled out. He hadn't come. He commanded Cuthwin to present his arse once more. The younger boy turned and collapsed his chest to the floorboards, his reddened buttocks up where they could easily be assaulted again.

'Let's see how much of a man you are,' Morgan growled at Denton. 'Put this over your filthy prick and get yourself into his arse.'

Denton rolled the thin rubber over his aching erection and knelt by Cuthwin's backside. He found the tight hole with his finger and pushed into it. His skin tingled slightly as the boy's hot body tightened around it. Morgan's belt came crashing down over his shoulders and he yelled.

'I said fuck him. Can't you do anything you're told? You're useless, you pathetic bastard! Fuck his arse or I'll take the skin off your back with my whip.'

Denton pressed his cock against the small, hot ring of muscle and pushed. The sphincter yielded and swallowed his meat. He could feel the pulsating walls of Cuthwin's passage, gripping and releasing – swallowing. Morgan's belt cracked across his shoulders once more and he began to buck and push. He knelt over the boy's body, his own larger frame exactly duplicating the one beneath him.

Morgan laughed and placed himself over the two of them. He was standing now, legs astride. Denton could tell that he was wanking himself over them. They might have been two animals fucking each other without regard to anyone who might be watching. Denton's desires raced around his head. He wanted to be beaten. He wanted to have that cruel, sarcastic, beautiful creature whip him as he had threatened to do.

45

Somehow pain was the only thing that would satisfy the burning inside his heart. He dared to ask for it.

'Please, sir. Punish me as you said you would. I deserve to be whipped, sir. Don't show me any mercy. Hurt me.'

'You really are a disgusting sniveller, aren't you?'

Morgan had stopped wanking and Denton slowed his own rhythm down in case he should come before he was allowed the agonising kiss of the whip.

It was not denied him. The flat, warming smacks of the belt were replaced by thin, piercing cuts. Although he couldn't see it, Denton knew he was being lashed with a horsewhip. The biting lashes across his back and the snug warmth around his cock sent his brain reeling in exquisite confusion. His balls contracted and shot his semen into the slave's backside with a force he had never before experienced. His body went limp and the whipping stopped.

He lay there while Morgan wanked over him. The splashes of semen hit him all over, from his neck to his coccyx. Satisfied grunts signalled the master was spent.

'Get off him.'

He pulled out of Cuthwin and removed the sheath from his prick. Morgan held out his hand for it.

Cuthwin, still bound, still hard, remained where he was. Morgan pushed him with his foot and he rolled on to his back. His smaller, thinner penis stood up from his body.

Morgan took the sheath and emptied its contents over his slave's chest. Cuthwin pushed his torso upward as if this would result in more of the pungent juices covering him. Morgan stood over his supine body and obliged his slave by spitting on his face and chest. He then squatted and used the boy's skin to wipe the come from his own, now flaccid, cock. Then he withdrew.

'Wank him off,' he commanded.

Denton knelt beside the lad and took as much care as he could to ensure the boy derived pleasure from his touch. He stroked and pulled, kneading the blood-gorged flesh with his fingertips. Cuthwin writhed and twisted then began to pant through the gag. His eyes grew wide, then shut tightly. He grimaced and spluttered into the material, and soon his open mouth became visible through it with the force of his intake of breath. His body suddenly relaxed completely and his breathing calmed. Denton wiped the come from his hand into the mess on the boy's skin. Morgan joined them and, surprisingly, kissed Denton in a loving and tender way.

'You can undo him. He's fulfilled his purpose,' he said.

Denton released Cuthwin, who remained where he was on the floor.

'If you want to take him to your bed, you can. I've had enough for one night,' Morgan said dismissively. 'Bring him back in the morning.'

With that he climbed into bed and turned away from them, apparently unconcerned with what they decided to do. Denton looked at the inviting body which had just been offered him. Knowing the answer before he asked the question he asked, 'Do you want to?'

Cuthwin simply nodded and rose to his feet. He waited by the door and then followed Denton back to the other bedroom.

The landlord had provided a bowl for washing and a jug of water. Denton cleaned himself and then offered the water to Cuthwin.

'I'm not allowed to,' he said. 'I have to let it stay on me until my master decides I should be washed.'

Denton climbed into bed.

'I'll fuck you again in the morning. Is that allowed?'

'I am yours for as long as my master has no need of me. I have no rights over my body. He owns me and he has given me to you.'

Denton wanted to ask questions but he suspected they would

47

not be answered. He pulled back the blanket and indicated for the slave to get into bed beside him. The boy obeyed.

Soon Denton was asleep. He awoke in the night to find Cuthwin curled up beside him, one slender arm around his chest, the other resting in between his legs. The light touch against Denton's cock made it hard again. He knew he could wake Cuthwin and satisfy himself but he decided not to. He would, he thought, wait until morning and do what he had to do then.

Cuthwin's closed eyelids flickered: dreams of what? Denton could only guess. Torture? Humiliation? Or love? Were they, perhaps, two parts of the same thing?

He put his own arm around the willing body and drifted into slumber.

Pascal

After that first, wonderful visit to his house when Casper had tied me to a table and fucked me, I knew I would not be able to stay away from his company for long. In fact, I visited him nearly every week up to the spring of that year. Each time I arrived, he would begin with polite, friendly conversation and then at some point suddenly decide it was time to switch to having sex. He would – sometimes when I was in mid-sentence – order me to take off my clothes, then he'd beat me and usually he would fuck me. Sometimes he didn't take me up the arse. He said he liked to think of me still wanting more. If he decided not to come himself, I wouldn't be allowed to either. When this happened he forbade me to masturbate until I saw him again.

'You must think of your prick as my property,' he told me once. 'It is not yours to touch unless you're given permission.'

It was difficult to obey this command. I would lie awake all night, my penis rigid and demanding. I would sometimes find myself stroking it, but my subservience was a real state of mind, not mere play-acting, and I always reminded myself my cock was mine no longer: it belonged to Caspar and I wasn't able to make free with his property.

This very denial stimulated me further. Because it was largely self-imposed (he surely would not have known if I'd indulged myself without his permission), it was my own private discipline and I always obeyed it. When we eventually met and he quizzed me – as he always did – I was proud to answer truthfully that I had been obedient and done as he had ordered. I had kept myself until permitted to do otherwise.

I made no moves to contact Troy. I thought it would be a useless exercise and I was getting all the sexual activity I wanted. I sometimes thought of him. I remembered what Caspar had said about seeing him tied up as I often was myself. Once or twice I confessed my thoughts to Caspar. He repeated that it was perfectly possible for me to have Troy in any way I wanted but he told me I mustn't do so without his, Caspar's, permission. Every time Troy was mentioned I had a sense of Caspar scheming in some way. He would smile knowingly and imply in what he said that something (I had no clue as to what) would eventually happen to bring my fantasies to life.

I retained a fond hope of arriving to find that my master had procured Troy for me. I could visualise myself turning up at his door and he would be there with Caspar. As was always the case with Caspar, they would be talking socially, with no hint of the sex that would surely follow. When it was time, Troy would obey Caspar's commands as readily as I. We would be naked together and then . . .

It was only a dream. I was able to content myself with what I actually had. If there was something missing, perhaps it was necessary it should be so. If Caspar had once professed love for me, would it be possible still to regard him as my owner? Somehow I doubted it. Love would necessitate equality and our lust was based on his superiority.

★　★　★

One day I was surprised to find Caspar did not want to sit and talk but suggested instead we went for a walk out of doors. I was disappointed. My cock had been pushing against my underwear since early morning. I was aware of a growing patch of pre-come oozing from its tip. I had hoped to be naked without too much delay, bound and plugged with Caspar's wonderful prick. A walk would be difficult with this unsatisfied desire on my mind. However, I didn't question him. I simply followed him out of the house and down the path.

'We're going to the wood over at the foot of the hill,' he told me. 'I know you're aching for my body. Be patient. You won't have to keep your cock under control for very long.'

The woods were dense and green. A thick carpet of bracken cushioned our footsteps. Caspar seemed to know where he was going although there was no discernible path. After ten minutes or so we stopped. He turned to me and told me, as he often did, to trust him.

I nodded eagerly. This was something new. I didn't know what he was going to do, but I sensed his growing ardour and knew that what would follow would prove to be every bit as good as being belted and fucked in his house.

He blindfolded me, using a tight, rubber mask which shut out all possibility of peripheral vision. Then he bound my hands together in front of me. He undid my white shirt and pulled it off my shoulders slightly. My chest was thus exposed to the cool breeze that licked around my back causing the shirt to billow out, revealing most of my naked chest.

I felt a tug on the rope: he had left enough loose to lead me where he wanted. I stumbled after him, wary of unseen obstacles in my path, but confident enough to know he would not let me hurt myself.

When we arrived at our destination, he steadied my body and told me to stand where I was and wait. I lowered my tightly bound hands and listened for further instruction. Being

51

only partly clothed made me more acutely aware of the degradation that bondage produced. My clothing was simply there to be stripped from my body. My shirt, pulled half off me as it was, at once reminded me I was a man, capable of covering my nudity, but at the same time it displayed my vulnerable, naked chest and showed me to be a prisoner whose body was in the complete control of another. My nipples were erect and sensitive. As the wind blew the cotton against my skin, they responded to its touch with a tingling which was as tangible as the touch of a man's hand.

Caspar rendered me further humiliation by undoing the front of my breeches and pulling the flaps away from my abdomen. I knew my genitals were still covered, but, like my upper body, they were made ready to be handled and I couldn't pretend any dignity.

'I like to see you this way,' he said quietly. 'You're too willing sometimes – I know you are simply complying with what I want. I have decided to demonstrate to you what being naked is about.

'This – ' He gripped my cock tightly through the fabric. 'This is normally what a man hides from view. At present you have it covered as any other person walking the streets would, but, prepared as you are, you know it's only your own for as long as I let you keep it to yourself. You're still clothed, but not so much that it isn't easy to see what you would look like once everything has been stripped from you. You do follow what I'm saying, don't you?'

I was about to answer but another voice replied, 'Yes, master.'

This last question had been addressed to somebody else! I was being put on show! Somebody whom I didn't know was now seeing me, almost denuded, my hands tied in front me and a blindfold round my eyes. It was not somebody to whom I had willingly exposed my body. I was truly without status. I wanted to fall to my knees and display my wretchedness to this stranger. I wanted to throw away any shred of self-respect I might have left and declare myself to be nothing more than Caspar's plaything: not a free human being, but an object.

The unseen person had used the word 'master'. Did this mean his flesh was similarly ready to be exposed? Was he secured with ropes? Or with chains perhaps? When had he been brought here?

Caspar laid his hand on my shoulder and pressed me down to an upright kneeling position. I lowered my head like a convicted man before the execution block. I waited for the shirt to be torn from my back and I hoped to feel the kiss of my master's belt across my bare shoulders. Whatever this other person might think of himself, I knew I could debase myself more than he. I was more obedient, more willing, more slavish.

'I told you of Tarne,' Caspar said to me. 'I told you of a community of men who lived there. One of them is with us now. Let me tell you something more about how they live their lives and why it was I suggested you go there one day.'

He knelt beside me and put his hand inside my shirt, round my back. He stroked me absently as he spoke, again displaying that strange mixture of lover and captor which I had come to associate with him.

'Mankind is taught to walk upright on two legs. We are told we are the superior animal on this planet. We give ourselves all sorts of airs and graces. We even cover our natural state with clothing, shy of letting others look on the reproductive organs or the anus. The higher up the human scale one goes, the more apparel one wraps around oneself. For example, only a privileged few will have ever seen the nipples of a king. To expose these means you're a lowly thing, even a slave – or perhaps another man's prisoner.'

He took my nipple between his finger and thumb, rolling it and squeezing. With his other hand he pulled my shirt more off my back. It fell to my elbows and I felt him run his fingers

53

over my shoulders and down the line of my neck to the top part of my spine.

'So,' he went on, 'we are given the illusion of respectability, of worth, of rights over our wretched bodies, which we decorate so they cannot be recognised for what they are. Despite all this, part of each one of us desires to cast aside the responsibility which accompanies the façade. Part of us wants to be the naked child we were when we came into this world. You, I know, would happily consent to abandoning every vestige of human privilege and agree to living the life of an animal with myself as your keeper. Your most sacred part – the hole where you shit – has already been defiled by me. I have put my cock into it and used it to waste my sperm in your bowels. You have nothing left now – there is no lower place I could take you. I thought I might use you to attract another to us. That is still a possibility, but I see you are not going to be active in seeking him out as I hoped you would. I have decided, therefore, to give you away, at least for a time. You have put yourself in my keeping and I am going to hand you over to another. You have no chance of escape; no appeal can be made against this decision. I have brought you here to understand that you must accept this.'

He let go of my nipple and moved away for a brief moment. Then I felt cold metal touch one of my biceps. It was some sort of steel ring he was fastening around me. I heard it click into place and lock – I supposed he used a key: certainly I knew it was going to remain there until he chose to remove it.

'This is engraved with my name,' he said. 'It is to show you are my property, below human consideration. If you ever try to deny it, to pretend you have a choice in what might happen to you, it will be there to prove you a liar. You are to be taken to Tarne. If you give yourself ridiculous notions of escape, you will be found out by this slave's band and taken back to where you will suffer castigation for your audacity. I told you I would help you understand what nakedness means. This is the first lesson. You are more naked with this band on your arm than you would ever be without it.'

My heart was thumping from fear and from excitement. I knew it was not my place to speak but, had I been given permission, I would have told him how much I wanted to crawl in the filth before his feet – to lick and kiss the dirt he walked on. I was nothing.

'You no longer have the right to wear this shirt,' Caspar said. His voice was still calm and reasonable. It betrayed no emotion of any kind.

He tore the shirt away from me. I heard it rip and I shivered, not from cold, but from anticipation.

He pulled my trousers further down, still keeping my penis inside the material. My hips and my buttocks were now exposed. He carried on talking:

'It's a good enough body to satisfy. Your skin is still young and smooth. How old are you?'

'Twenty, sir,' I said. My own voice sounded unnatural to me, as though it belonged to someone else.

'That's right. Twenty. It's a good age to learn servitude. This other person who is watching you – he is nearly thirty. He has been owned by men since he was your age. I want you to follow his example and be a good slave. He will teach you how to please your new masters. He will show you how to sublimate your impudent desire to satisfy your own lust, to accept that you deserve a whip around your back more than a lover's arms. It's time for you to see what you will become.'

He removed the blindfold from my eyes, slowly, carefully. I blinked as the light hit me. We were in a clearing, surrounded by tall pines and cedars. In the centre of this was an oak which had low branches.

The man was shackled to the trunk of this venerable tree. His chains were fixed with rivets into the wood. The only covering he had been allowed was a loose, ill-fitting piece of linen around his loins. It was low down on his stomach,

55

showing the top of his bush of golden pubic hair. This graduated upward into a thin but defined line which spread again when it reached his navel. Above, it trailed the centre of his chest, nestling under his pectoral muscles and touching lightly round the dark peaks which surmounted them. His Adam's apple was pronounced in his slender neck and his jaw was underlined by a trimmed beard. He had thick, kissable lips, slightly open to show a set of gleaming white teeth. His nose was slightly overlong – but very slightly. It didn't spoil the beauty of his pale, blue eyes, which gazed upon me sadly and kindly as though he understood my plight and was sorry for it. He had been shaved close to his scalp, but the remaining hair was of the same golden colour as that on his body.

He wore heavy chains around his ankles, his wrists and his neck. Each length was linked to the others, forming a crisscross web of iron in front of his body. The links extended beyond him and were fastened well into the tree allowing him a few short feet of movement only. He, like me, wore a band around his arm. It was, as I assumed mine to be, of gleaming steel and was engraved with words I could not read. His legs, spattered with mud, were densely covered with curly hair which caught the sun here and there, turning the yellow to shining silver.

'This is André. He has been chosen to be your special companion on the journey you will make. He is owned by the masters of Tarne, as are you from this moment on. They will be coming here to claim you later tonight. Are you prepared for what will happen, Pascal?'

'Yes, sir. I am prepared.' I was transfixed by the beauty of the slave before me. I felt unworthy. My own poor looks seemed as nothing by comparison.

'I will show you how you will be when they come for you. Stand up.'

I did as I was told. My breeches fell to the ground. My aching cock sprang free and I noticed André immediately fixing upon it. His fetters allowed him access to his own groin, but he merely pressed his hands into his inner thighs. Presumably he was under orders not to touch his cock until permission was granted.

Caspar unbuttoned his shirt, maybe because of the warm air, but maybe because he knew how much the black fur on his chest made me melt. He knelt and brushed some leaves away from something which lay on the ground between me and the chained slave.

'Step out of your breeches. You have no right to them any more. Come over here and lift this wood.'

I obeyed. The wood he spoke of was a thick pole about nine or ten feet long. It had been chiselled to give it a flat aspect and I immediately noticed an iron ring driven into it near the top.

'There's a place for it in the ground near to where its foot is,' Caspar told me.

It was extremely heavy and I struggled to keep it upright. Where Caspar had indicated, there was a deep hole, its circumference just about wide enough to accommodate the wooden post. I heaved the thing nearly into place and, after some minutes of clumsy manoeuvring, it fell home. The hole was some few feet deep, holding it secure and upright, leaving enough above ground to accommodate my full height with my hands shackled above me.

'I see you already know how I am to leave you to await your fate,' Caspar smiled. 'You will find it erotic for maybe an hour or so, but your owners will not arrive until much later this evening. By that time your arms will be aching. Your prick will not have been relieved and it will therefore still be erect. You will make a fine sight for those who have bought you.'

I must have looked up as he spoke this last sentence. He nodded.

'Yes, you have been sold. I told you that you belonged to me. You agreed to it often enough. Every man has a right to sell what is his. Unless, that is, the man is such a kind as you and this beautiful wretch here, for slaves don't own anything. But I don't think you fully understand your nakedness yet, do you?'

I mumbled that I did – I thought. He quietened me.

'No, you don't. There's further to take you. Come towards me.'

I approached him and he put both his hands either side of my face. He pushed back into my hair and let it trail through his fingers. Then he brought his hands down to my cock and combed through my pubes. His intentions now became perfectly clear. The hair on my body was still covering me. I was not fully nude.

'You're going to take my hair from me,' I said. 'I am to be shaved.'

'Your silky, brown locks and your thick, lovely pubes. The soft velvet round your shithole and that fine bush under your armpits. Such vanity to want it still! You have no need of it, boy. In time, they may allow you to grow it back on your body, but not on your head. I told them you were too arrogant for that. You must be penitent, you must have a constant reminder of what you are. Kneel as you were before, with your head down so I can take away your hair.'

I sobbed. He knew I was proud of it. He knew I felt it made me more handsome, more appealing. I was to go into my life of slavery looking like a criminal. I was not even to be allowed to keep the hair round my arsehole. I knelt before him and lowered my head. He undid my hands briefly before tying them again, this time behind my back so I couldn't interfere with his appalling act. André was watching intently. I wondered if he had been shaved all over when he was first captured. Would they allow me my body hair back as they had evidently allowed him his?

Caspar took a knife from his belt. He must have had it there all along, but I hadn't seen it. It was razor sharp. He began to hack away at my head hair. Soon most of it was on the ground in front of my eyes. He then took a blade from a small bag he had brought with him and scraped at my scalp until I knew there was nothing left but fine stubble.

He kicked me lightly in the chest with the toe of his boot and I fell on to my back. He pushed my legs apart and applied the razor carefully round my cock and balls. The scraping against my skin was a pleasant enough feeling, but the visual result was horrifying to me. In a few short minutes I was like a newborn baby. My penis looked a ridiculous thing without its mane. I was reminded of my teenage embarrassment when my schoolfellows, most of them already adult men between their legs, had laughed at my childish loins. I had tried to cover myself: then I was able to, now I could not. My legs were wide apart and my nude sexual organs were exposed totally.

When Caspar was satisfied with his work, he lifted my legs into the air and took the razor to my arse. Again, the sensation was pleasant and he did at least take care not to cut me, but to have to submit to this indignity was almost as much as I could take. He took a longer time over the area round my hole than he had with the rest of my buttocks. I think he must have just enjoyed looking at that most private of places.

Finished, he told me to stand.

'I'll place you as they said you were to be. Then I'll complete your shame by removing the evidence of manhood from your armpits. It'll be easier for me once your arms are chained above you. Get against the post.'

Once more, my hands were freed briefly and once more they were fixed. Caspar produced heavy metal handcuffs from his bag. This time I was manacled to the iron ring. My arms were pulled up above my head, not totally stretched, but far enough to expose my poor armpits.

It didn't take long. When he'd done, he busied himself for a short time with the fine hair on my chest. Then he was finished.

I understood at last what it was to be totally naked. From

that day to the present, I never experienced such an aching emotion as I felt then. I was crying quite openly. This of course only added to my abjectness. Still André had not been permitted to speak. Still he watched, his hands hovering around his now defined cock – but never touching it.

Caspar turned to him. 'This boy is not to be allowed to come. I, however, am going to shoot my sperm over him. I am going to because I have decided to. I am a master and you are slaves. That's the way of it.'

With that he pulled his shirt over his head and dropped his trousers. His thick cock was enormous – it could have been a hungry animal. He put his hand under the cloth around André's waist and found what was in there. André gasped and closed his eyes. Caspar played with him for a while, watching his reactions to the touch he wanted so much. I felt desperately needful of similar attention. I wondered if it would be possible to come without anyone touching me. If it were, surely this would be a time when it would happen. I had never known whether I was capable of it – when I had wet dreams I was never sure I hadn't wanked myself off as I slept.

And yet I was still the slave, still telling myself it was not my right even to desire release when it had been forbidden me so expressly. My masters wanted me to wait until they decided I could let go of my seed. If I felt as though I might orgasm without benefit of touch, then I must do all I could to prevent it and turn my thoughts to other things.

How could I? Caspar was wanking in front of me. André had been left, still clothed around his waist with his cock now standing proud within the white cotton that housed it. If he could restrain his desires, so could I.

Caspar stood even closer. He was looking down at the end of his cock with a kind of intense interest as if he was gazing down the entrance of some burrowed hole in the ground, waiting for a creature to emerge. He thrust his hips forward to make sure the semen that would surely be springing forth any second would spill over my shaven skin. His other hand ran hard through his own chest hair, underlining the fact that he had stolen mine from me.

Then he closed his eyes: rapturous. His head went back and he let out a deep sigh of utter contentment. The salty cream hit my stomach and immediately ran in small rivulets down to my tender groin. He pumped himself until it was all gone. Then he put his fingers in it and wiped a good deal of the stuff over my face.

He dressed quickly and, with a last cautionary look in my direction, he was gone.

I didn't know whether it was proper to speak. We were evidently able to do so and we hadn't been told we could not. We both stared at each other with huge, aching lust in our eyes. I marvelled at the wondrous body in front of me. At the same time I was mortified by my own pitiful state.

André spoke first. His voice was rounded and pleasant. (I hadn't really noticed its deep musical tones when, before, he had said those few words.)

'Are you ready for what is in store for you? Truly?' he asked.

'I think so,' I replied. I didn't know what further indignities awaited me; perhaps he did. Perhaps whatever was about to happen to me had already been done to him in the past.

'What do you want it to be?'

'I don't know. I was free to make my own decisions only a few hours ago. Now I am somebody else's property and I must obey their commands. Am I . . .'

I hesitated. I knew what I wanted to say but I didn't want to betray my desires. I felt I should have no pleasure in my fate. I almost hoped what was to come would be as difficult to take as the last hour had been.

'Speak,' he said. 'You might not be given the chance later.'

'Do you think they'll whip me?' I said. I felt stupid asking it. My tone was like that of a child pleading to be taken to the fair. I had meant it to be a serious question, imbued with the gravity such a cruel punishment seemed to merit.

'Yes, you will be whipped. And you will be fucked, and you will be brought even lower than you are now. Don't think of yourself as anything more than a piece of meat. You are no longer yourself. I am no longer myself. We are slaves. Before, you thought of all this as a game. It isn't. It's a way of life.'

A way of life, I thought. Caspar had spoken of a method for living. This was the secret behind that badly painted landscape in Caspar's home. This was Tarne.

Two

Troy took another long draught of beer and immediately wished he hadn't. He felt sick. He was aware, just, that he looked as drunk as he felt. He had been sitting in a corner of the room all evening quietly drowning his sorrows. When he had been persuaded to attend this party (against his better judgment), he had been assured he would have a wonderful time and there would be hundreds of people lining up to meet him – all of them gorgeous; all of them available; all of them approachable. So far, no one had spoken to him at all. Even his friends, Spencer and Dino, had deserted him in favour of a long and boring conversation about politics.

Whatever terrible character trait it was that condemned him to this solitary life remained a complete mystery to him. He had good looks. He exercised daily and made sure he always dressed well. He was not running to fat or losing his hair. In fact, many people had complimented him, some rather enviously, on his physical appeal. He was in his mid-twenties now and looked as though he was in his teens.

There had been a time when he wondered and worried if he might perhaps be effeminate, but he wasn't and he knew he wasn't. Having long, shining hair and a baby face didn't mean he was any less the man. He had even analysed his walk, looking for any sign of prissiness, and had found nothing to reproach himself for.

He was good company, too, when he was given the chance to be. He could engage in humorous conversation and usually managed to win friends easily. The only trouble was, they had to approach him. He never dared to make the first move. He hated parties. They always ended in his sitting like he was now, ignored and alone. Everyone seemed to be having a good time apart from him and it wasn't fair.

Spencer had told him that maybe his bad luck was down to his being so desperate. Perhaps he gave an impression of being clingy, of wanting to jump into a full-blown relationship with whoever he was speaking to, before they'd had a chance to get to know him. This might be true, he mused.

He didn't feel he was the sort who would leap into bed with just anyone. He was actually rather choosy. He liked men, not women, and he liked his men to be older than he was – slightly. He liked them to be dominant and sure of themselves. He liked them to be all the things he wasn't.

At the moment, 'the things he wasn't' included being sober. The alcohol helped to make the hours pass, but it also made him miserable and, he was well aware of it, made him the sort of person any sensible soul would avoid.

Earlier, a pleasant sort of man, who appeared also to be on his own, had spoken to him briefly. He'd smiled and asked if Troy was all right. Was he enjoying himself? Troy had immediately launched into a slurred and ververbal life history which had sent the potential friend scurrying away as quickly as he had arrived. Troy had kicked himself as he always did, and lapsed back into his own private world.

He'd hoped he would have made something of himself by now. He had hated his home life and had now successfully abandoned it. His mother and father could go to hell as far as he was concerned. They were no longer a part of him and he was nothing to do with them. He was going to be happy and he was going to be free.

He had covered his tracks absolutely. It was pretty certain that his family supposed him to have lost his reason and joined some religious cult in a village some way from where he had actually chosen to live. In fact he knew nothing of Tarne or of the community that he had professed to have changed his life. He'd read about it somewhere and it seemed the perfect cover. There was no way his parents could, or would, try to find him there. They would assume he was lost to them for ever and simply disown him. Thereby he had his escape and the added advantage of not suffering any guilt over leaving them wondering if he was alive or dead. Perfect.

The door opened and another band of revellers appeared. They were a cheerful bunch who appeared to know most of the people there. One of them immediately went over to Spencer and Dino and exchanged hugs and kisses. Maybe his friends would introduce him . . .? No, the other man had already excused himself and moved off into another corner of the room.

Troy rehearsed, as he so often did, going over to one of the newcomers and, taking care not to stagger or slur, asking them where they came from. What did they do for a living? In this scenario, the other always immediately became accommodating and within minutes was asking Troy where he lived and was he doing anything after the party? Troy mentally skipped a few hours and imagined being back at his own place or theirs, the bed inviting and obvious. They would perhaps play a game of cards which would end with forfeits – clothes being discarded. Troy always lost the game. He never actually wanted to win. The game not finished, they would put a higher stake on the last hand of cards. This would be an item of the opponent's clothing against Troy's body.

65

'If you lose, you're mine for the night, to do anything I want to.'

Troy felt his cock stir at the thought. It was one of his favourite fantasies. Needless to say, he would lose yet again and therefore be the other man's prize.

He was hazy about what would happen to him after that. He wanted the other person to take control of him, perhaps to fuck him. He'd never been fucked and he always wondered if it was better than when he was alone in his rooms, where he used some cock-shaped object to push into his hole and fill him while he wanked. It was often difficult to keep his hand going on his prick and, at the same time, keep the makeshift dildo thrusting effectively into his arse. A man would do both for him. He would just have to lie back and enjoy it.

The group that Spencer and Dino had joined shifted to allow three others to come in. One of them was a familiar face. Troy had seen him at another party he had attended some months ago. He had jet-black hair and pale skin. He had those looks that one would associate with a poet or a musician who used himself perhaps a little too much, but whose ravaged appearance was romantic and still appealing. His eyes were particularly so. He seemed more alive than anyone around him because of them. They shone with a bright intensity which gave his face an intelligent, immediate quality. From where he was sitting it was clear to Troy that this man could make the person he was talking to feel like the only person in the world.

Again the mental scenario lurched into its preliminary stages. Troy going over and saying something like, 'Haven't we met before?'

It was no good. He couldn't do it, so what was the point of thinking about it? It only made him feel more isolated. He would have maybe another drink, or two, then he would go home. With just a little more poison in his system, he would be able to forget all about everything until morning. Then he knew he would regret the indulgences of the previous evening and worry all day about who had seen him in that condition and who would be talking about it. It was the way it always happened.

He finished what he had in his glass and rose unsteadily to his feet. The refreshment, as Spencer had called it, was laid out on a table in another room. He would therefore have to negotiate his way through the crowd and hopefully not fall over before he reached it.

He didn't manage it. His head swam and he tripped over nothing. Blackness descended. It wasn't the first time.

When he awoke it was nearly dawn. He could tell hours had passed because of the quality of the light. He was in a small room at the top of a house. The wall sloped down to the floor and a small window showed nothing but the lightening sky. The floor was covered with thick rugs and the bed on which he had been laid was hard, but comfortable.

Panic immediately overwhelmed him. Maybe he was still in the place where the party had been held and he would have to confront his hosts. He would have to explain he wasn't used to drink and this was such an unusual occurrence that it would have to be laughed off and forgiven just this once. They wouldn't believe him of course because Dino and Spencer would already have told them that he was always doing this. He was a liability and he wouldn't be asked again.

Why bother about that? he asked himself. He didn't know these people and he didn't want to be invited to any more lonely nights sitting on the edge of a crowd of people enjoying themselves.

He had to piss. He tried to hold it in because finding a lavatory would mean exposing himself to the danger of meeting somebody. The demands of Mother Nature were too much. He told himself it was too early for anyone else to be about and he would be safe. In any case he had no choice. If he didn't piss in a lavatory he would do it in the bed and that would be far worse than anything.

He pulled back the covers and found that he was almost naked. He still had his underwear on, but that was all. His clothes were in a neat pile on the floor beside the bed. Somebody had had to undress him.

He swore to the gods he would never touch another drop of strong liquor. He knew he was lying.

The door opened onto a corridor. There was a flight of stairs leading down to the main part of the building but no other rooms on that floor. He tried to be very quiet, wishing he had bothered to put a shirt around him before attempting this mission.

On the floor below he found what he was looking for. There was a room with a sunken bathing pool and, just off it, there was a raised platform of the sort that had been in vogue a few years earlier. The edges of the latrine were covered in a ring of warm fur. Troy sat and let go of his piss, thinking how good it felt when he really needed to urinate. He let it flow out of him in a strong, satisfying stream.

At the side of the lavatory there was a bucket for flushing. He filled it from the tap on the wall and poured it down the well. He sat again and put his head in his hands, thinking what to do next.

He could run upstairs, get dressed and sneak out before anybody came to find him. Though this might solve his immediate problems, it would surely make him feel racked with guilt for days. A note would be enough to excuse him. That was it! He would leave a note, thanking the person or persons for their kindness and apologising for his behaviour. After all, he'd only passed out. He hadn't been violent or abusive as he had seen others be in similar conditions. He began to feel better.

Without considering how on earth he was going to get home, or even what he would do if, once on the road outside, he didn't know where he was, he left the bathing chamber and began to climb the stairs back to the roof.

'You've recovered, then,' said a voice below.

Standing behind him, looking up from a lower landing, was the man who he'd recognised the previous night. He was wearing a long robe which was open, revealing a hairy body clothed underneath only in a pair of white trunks. He had not long been out of bed for his black hair was tousled and those wonderful eyes blurry from sleep.

'My name's Caspar,' he said. 'I believe you're Troy.'

Troy pushed his plate aside and smiled. He had not said very much and neither had Caspar. There seemed to be an unspoken understanding that conversation should wait until they were both fully awake.

Caspar had made some herbal drink which had done Troy's head the world of good. He was feeling far more himself now. The paranoia that usually overtook him after a night's drinking had all but vanished. Caspar didn't seem to mind that he had fallen over, or that he had had to be put to bed. He even confessed to having been in the same state himself only a week or so before.

'You didn't seem to be having the best of times of it last night,' he said at last. 'Spencer is a nice man, but he won't look after people properly. I take it you didn't know anyone there?'

Troy nodded.

'I've seen you before at a party, last autumn. You didn't seem to have anyone with you then either. Do you always go to gatherings on your own?'

'I wasn't on my own,' Troy protested. 'Spencer and his boyfriend, Dino – they were with me. It's just they fell into conversation with other people.'

Caspar came and stood by the back of Troy and began to massage his shoulders absently. It felt good. Troy succumbed to the unfamiliar contact and leant back, his eyes closed.

'Tell me if it hurts,' Caspar said. 'You're very tense.'

Neither of them had bothered to get dressed yet. Troy had been lent a robe, similar to the one Caspar himself was wearing. It was good to wander around a house with so little clothing on. It felt almost like the two of them were lovers and had spent the night together. Troy, his imagination always present to fill in the pieces life denied him, had let this be his fantasy all the way through breakfast. The firm touch of Caspar's able fingers on his knotted shoulder muscles was the perfect adjunct to the invention.

Caspar pulled the gown off Troy's back and went down further. Troy pushed the used crockery on the table well out of harm's way and lay forward on his folded arms, slipping the robe off completely as he did so.

'No,' Caspar said. 'That's enough now. My hands will get tired if I go on and we wouldn't want that, would we?'

He said this suggestively. Or maybe Troy was just imagining it. Dare he respond? He wanted to say something but couldn't find the right words. It was always the thing that stopped him getting what he wanted. He just didn't have the courage to ask for what he needed. On the other hand, that the man was good-looking, friendly and willing to give him a massage didn't mean he was also willing to take Troy into his bed. If Troy said anything he might be rejected. He might even meet with a hostile reaction. He had no way of telling.

'I remember you from last autumn. I noticed you,' Troy said. 'I wanted to speak to you, but you were with someone.'

A knowing smile spread over Caspar's face. 'Yes, I remember. I was, wasn't I? I don't think I'll be seeing him for some time. He's away from home and nobody seems to know when he might be back.'

'He seemed very nice,' Troy said.

'Would it interest you to know he wanted to talk to you, just as much as you might have wanted to talk to me?'

Troy sat upright again. There could be no mistaking the

implications of what his new friend was saying. The smile had not left Caspar's face. He seemed to be keeping something back and it seemed to be increasingly obvious what it was.

Troy now had another dilemma to contend with. If he confessed he had been just as attracted to the mystery person as he had been to Caspar, it might result in his losing his chances now. Yet, if he said nothing, he might be missing the possibility of getting to know someone who genuinely felt attracted to him.

'You do like me, don't you?' Caspar asked.

'You mean . . .'

This was pathetic! It was all about as obvious as it could be and still he didn't have the strength just to say it.

'Yes, I mean . . .' Caspar mimicked him. 'I know there are those of us who prefer the opposite sex. It does happen. Even when they are as attractive as you are.'

It was now or never. He had said enough to give Troy the confidence to be open about everything. For the first time in his life he decided to throw caution to the winds.

'I want to be with a man very much indeed, but I never have. You're very beautiful and I wish you'd . . .'

He gulped. This was it. He would do it.

'I wish you'd play a game of cards with me. The prize would be my body or yours depending on which of us loses our clothing first. Does that sound very stupid?'

'I have a better idea,' Caspar said. He disappeared and came back with an empty bottle in his hand. 'Cards take too long for my liking,' he explained. 'How about spinning this a few times. It has the same effect. And no,' he added. 'I don't think it's stupid. It's a wonderful idea.'

They sat on the floor, the bottle between them. Caspar insisted they put on three more garments and slippers too. This would give the game a bit more of an edge, he suggested.

They spun; Troy first. The neck of the bottle came to rest

in between them, pointing at neither. Caspar's turn: this time it pointed directly at Troy.

He removed a slipper. He wanted to dispense with the robe – he wanted to get down to his underwear as quickly as possible – but the slipper would have to do for now.

The next go fell to Caspar as he'd won the last one. This time it worked against him and he also removed one of his slippers.

Troy spun again and once more it pointed at Caspar. He took off his other slipper and grinned.

'Beginner's luck,' he concluded. 'I'll soon have you, don't you worry.' He thought for a moment. 'I suppose we ought to decide what the rules are when one or the other of us loses.'

'That they forfeit themselves to the winner,' Troy said simply.

'How much? I mean, if you lost, would you be prepared to do whatever I wanted you to? Or are you expecting something which you're hoping I'll coincidentally want as well? You might not like what I have in mind.'

'What do you have in mind?'

He wouldn't say. Troy, who was by now utterly captivated, recklessly agreed to do anything that was asked of him. Caspar nodded slowly.

'And I also agree to that,' he said. 'If you win, I'll be whatever you wish me to be.'

The game proceeded. Soon Troy was able to take off not only the scarf, the hat, the pants, but also the robe. He was almost naked. Only his underwear covered him. He was pleased with his body and noticed with growing satisfaction that Caspar looked him over intently and seemed to appreciate what he saw.

Then, things went the other way and Caspar had to divest himself of one item of apparel after another. It wasn't long before both men were down to underwear and the crucial spin would decide which of them it was to be.

To Troy's absolute disappointment, the bottle came to rest pointing squarely at Caspar.

There was a long and meaningful silence. Caspar eventually got up and gestured for Troy to do the same.

'You've won,' he said. 'I'm yours. Do you know what you want to do with me?'

Troy shook his head. 'I'm not sure. I didn't expect to win.'

'We agreed what the rules would be. We must abide by them now or the game will have no point. For a start, you might like to have the privilege of making me naked.'

With trembling hands, Troy reached for the belt of Caspar's trunks and pulled slowly downward. He had seen naked men before of course, but only in situations where he had to steal occasional glances. Never had he been so close to someone, and someone to whom he knew he could do anything he wanted.

Caspar had a stomach like a slab of rock. His black pubic hair bushed out over the top of his underwear. Each small tug produced yet more of it. He watched Troy's face the whole time, his hands compliantly by his sides.

His cock was huge. It was trapped, pointing downward, and, once released, it bounced completely the other way, almost reaching his navel. His balls hung loose and heavy beneath. Troy edged the garment down his strong legs and Caspar stepped free of it. He stood – waiting.

'You're very beautiful,' Troy said. 'I don't know what to do.'

'I told you the rules demanded I be anything you want me to be,' Caspar replied. 'That means anything. Do you understand?'

Troy shook his head. There must be some fantasy which Caspar wanted him to enter into, but he didn't know what it was and he wasn't experienced enough to find out.

73

'I'll make it easy for you,' Caspar explained. 'I think you wanted to lose the game, am I right?'

He didn't wait for an answer.

'If I am, that means you want me to be the instigator of what we do together. That's all right. I can be anything you want me to be,'

'Do it,' Troy said. 'Please, I'm no good at this. You be the one who says what is to happen.'

Caspar took him in his arms and kissed him roughly. His breath smelt of stale beer but it was a manly, erotic taste and Troy loved it. His tongue went easily into Caspar's mouth and he melted. Then, to his great surprise, Caspar pulled back and slapped him across the face.

'Get my cock into your mouth and suck it,' he ordered.

Troy was confused and suddenly scared. He had expected slow, passionate lovemaking. Not daring to do otherwise, he did as he was told.

It was the first time a man's penis had been in his mouth. It was hot and slightly sweaty. The smell of sex filled Troy's nostrils and he was soon lost to the world. Caspar stood immobile, watching him. There was a salty taste in Troy's mouth – it masked another, more delicate flavour which he supposed to be the stuff that had so often stained his own pants. He sucked it in and it became more intense.

'It's still your game,' Caspar said, 'You can carry on doing this and you can say how far you want it to go. Or you can give yourself to me completely. If you do, it might take the rest of the day and even until tomorrow. It will be difficult for you, but I think you'll enjoy it. Which is it to be?'

Troy reluctantly let go of his prize and looked into Caspar's blue eyes. There was still that intensity there, still that beauty, but underneath there was something else. It was a coldness that thrilled Troy and scared him at the same time. Gradually he became aware of what was being asked of him. He remembered the slap. That, too, had become eroticised in his mind.

'You want to hurt me?' he asked.

'No, I won't hurt you. It's your first time. But I might want to do things to you that you find difficult to take. I want to show you what it's like to belong to somebody else properly. I promise you'll be safe, but you'll have to do as you're told.'

Troy's cock overruled any doubts he might have. He was still clothed around his waist and he felt the material caress the head of his penis as it stirred in response to Caspar's words.

'I'll do it,' he answered.

He was taken to a windowless room which was bare of furniture. Running from one wall to the other, about three feet from the ground, a long pole divided the space in two. There was an array of handcuffs, rope, belts, straps and whips carelessly thrown on the floor as though some prisoner had just escaped leaving the evidence of his bondage and torture for others to find.

Caspar smiled and Troy noticed, for the first time, that his smile was not entirely pleasant. It was lascivious and predatory and it unnerved him. Even so, it found a response in Troy's cock, which jumped, wanting human touch. He reminded himself that Caspar had said he would not be hurt – 'it's your first time'. He almost volunteered to waive this condition, for the thought of being thrashed was tempting. Perhaps Caspar would go through the motions of flogging him without laying on the lash so much that it cut into his flesh.

'Kneel,' Caspar said brusquely. 'Hands on head.'

When he was in the required position, Caspar came and stood very close to Troy. Troy looked up at the beautiful body towering above him and was rewarded for this by a gob of saliva across his face.

'Did I say you could look at me?'

Troy lowered his eyes. This was not enough to expiate his mistake. Caspar pushed him roughly with his foot so that he had to lean back on his haunches, his back almost flat to the floor. He tried to keep his hands on his head, but he could not. Caspar placed his bare foot next to Troy's lips.

'Kiss my foot and show me how sorry you are.'

Troy kissed it as though it were the lips of an eastern prince. He licked under Caspar's heel and in between his toes. He sucked on each toe, loving the solid, hard skin in his mouth and revelling in the faint taste of sweat.

Caspar stepped back and motioned for Troy to continue his work in a more accessible way. Troy crawled towards him and willingly serviced his master's other foot as he had the first. His hands found their place on the back of his head; all his emotions seemed to gravitate towards the throbbing expectancy at the end of his penis. Grovelling, making love to the feet of this dark and hairy beauty, it seemed like his every wish had been fulfilled.

'Stand,' Caspar told him eventually. 'Put your arms behind the bar and bring your hands to the front of your body.'

Thus Troy was secured. His hands were chained in front of his chest. The bar held him, running across the small of his back and through the bend of his arms. It was not a difficult posture to maintain and Troy was able to gaze on his own chained wrists and consider his abject, naked state. It was more than he could have hoped for. Suddenly he wanted to throw himself once more at this man's feet and declare himself to be the lowest thing in creation. He wanted to show a willingness to accept whatever ignominy he must if only he could serve this wonderful master. His heart swelled with a passion he had never before known and he gave way to his tears, which were the expression of it.

'It is my habit to leave my slaves for a while. It will be good for you to have to wait until I decide to fuck your hole. So you must understand what I am offering you. Do you understand?'

'Yes, sir,' Troy whispered.

'Tell me.'

'You're offering to make me your servant, sir. You're offering me the honour of being the rag you wipe the dirt from your body with. I am to be your naked slave and my will no longer belongs to me.'

He said all this in halting gasps, too glutted with lust to be able to articulate normally. The words themselves added to his state of exquisite tension. They were voiced in response to Caspar, but Troy knew they were for his own benefit. He knew that, from that day onward, he would never be able to express sexual love fully unless it was to be like this.

Caspar smiled and kissed him slowly.

'Good boy,' he said in a low, confidential voice. 'You are perfect for my needs. I shall enjoy preparing you for what is to come.'

He let saliva drop from his lips on to Troy's face once again. This time it wasn't to show disapproval, it was a bonding – as though he needed to mark Troy with his own fluid. He smoothed the spittle into his prisoner's skin passing it gently over Troy's features – even his eyelids.

Troy breathed in deeply and yearned to be taken close to Caspar's body. He wanted most of all to be bound and caressed at one and the same time. He wanted to sleep with those muscular, male arms holding him close while ropes bit into his own wrists and chains around his neck and ankles reminded him of his lowly state.

Caspar seemed to read his mind.

'In time, it will all happen. For now you must reflect. I will come for you when I am ready.'

He left the room and Troy was alone, but, for the first time since he could remember, he was happy.

Pascal

It was some hours before the Superiors came to collect us from the woods. André had not said much. He regarded me quietly, taking in my poor, shaved body and clearly finding pleasure in what he saw, though his hand never went too close to his cock.

My discomfort was ameliorated by the desire that pulsed through me. When I was little more than a child, I had had a picture of some hero of old who had been taken in battle and had been tortured. He was shown in chains, in a similar position to the one in which I had been left. His hands had been yanked up above him and his torso was covered in sweat. He wore trousers of course and his skin sported reddish-brown body hair, but the whip marks across his chest and the look of hunted pathos in his eyes had made me yearn to be as he was. I had sometimes posed in front of a mirror, my hands raised, my wrists just out of the reflection so their untied state would not be allowed to spoil the illusion. When my cock was hard I had punished it until my balls let go and I could clear my head once more – until the next time I reached under my bed and brought the picture out. Now my dream had come true, more so than I could have hoped for then.

Four of them arrived eventually. One was especially attractive to me, though they were all handsome. He was in his mid- to late twenties and, like the others who had arrived with him, was dark and hirsute. He wore a tiny golden earring in his left lobe and, with his long black hair, deep green eyes and swarthy complexion, he could easily have been a gypsy or even a pirate.

I imagined him to be the latter. He followed the dress code adopted by the others: open white shirt, knee-breeches, his feet and calves bare. On the others it seemed a smart attire, but on him it seemed wild and exotic. He carried himself with a panache which his friends didn't possess. His head was kept high and he walked with a swagger as though he had a sword at his side and was ready to do battle with anyone who might dare to cross him. His name, I heard them say, was Leon.

His companions were all of similar type but they had not Leon's extra sexual bravado. One was a youngster, no more than eighteen or nineteen, but he was brawny beyond his years. The other two were of Leon's age. They didn't look exactly alike by any means: all were of different sizes and shapes, but with similar black hair and dark eyes. I might have believed them to be of one family. All four were dressed, as I was to come to realise, in the uniform clothes adopted by the Superiors of their community.

I think I must have fallen asleep in my bound state. André had, too, but the tread of bare feet on the bracken had woken him and the stirrings of his fetters had woken me.

The four Superiors carried two long poles between them. They had bags, one of which I noticed had rope trailing from its opening.

My fantasy of being led in chains to a life of slavery was about to come true, but it was going to be more than that. I guessed from what I saw that we were to be tied to the poles and carried back to Tarne like the carcasses of two animals.

First, I was to be examined. Leon was the one who did it. He squatted in front of me and took my cock between his finger and thumb as though he had found some interesting piece of flora. While he was doing this, another of them was releasing André from his chains.

Leon squeezed me and prodded underneath my balls. I hoped he might wank me – I wanted it desperately. He didn't.

'I need a piss,' he said. 'I wonder whether our new slave will make an acceptable lavatory for me?'

His voice was deep and he had a slight accent. The other three laughed and told him to carry on and not mind their presence. He fumbled at his belt and soon released a thin, long prick which had been circumcised and was not yet erect.

I had never been pissed on before. It had often been in my mind to ask Caspar to do it to me, but it hadn't been my place to dictate what should happen between us. Now to be so used was to accept utterly that I was a thing, property, no longer a man.

I dared to look at him as he spurted the first gush of yellow liquid over my chest. He met my eye and smiled crookedly. It was the first time I had been acknowledged at all and I felt my emotions clamour at my guts. Truth to tell, I think I would have given my heart, body and soul to just about any handsome young man who showed a willingness to take it.

He was like a small boy who took pride in the force of the stream he was able to produce. It came in several spurts, then in a constant high flow. He aimed it up, splashing my face and some of it entering my open mouth. I let my bonds take all the weight of my body: this was the very pinnacle of my needs and desires.

He seemed to have an unending amount of urine in his bladder. When my face and chest were dripping with it, he aimed at my cock directly. The concentrated force of the piss stimulated the head of my organ. I wanted it to last for ever.

The arc of liquid eventually collapsed and died. He came close to me and rubbed his fluid into my skin.

'You'll smell of me now, boy,' he said. 'You'll stink of my piss. Next time you'll get it all in your mouth and you'll drink it for me.'

I wanted to ask him to do that now. I wanted to drink his piss, to kiss his body, to feel his whip – anything. I had the sense to keep my thoughts to myself. Instead of speaking, I lowered my head respectfully.

'Right,' he called to the others. 'Let's get them ready to take back.'

André, by this time, was lying on his back. He was free of his chains, but he kept his hands above his head as if in a gesture of surrender. Two of the boys brought a pole and laid it across his middle. It extended beyond the extremities of his body. They tied him, wrist over wrist, ankle to ankle, and then to the pole itself. He was left in a foetal position, his golden hair still shining – a lion, denied his glory and prepared for slaughter.

I was cut down. I could support myself no longer. I simply collapsed, face downward, into the undergrowth. My arms throbbed from having been above me for so long, but they weren't to have much relief. In little more than a minute, I was trussed to my pole in the same way as André was to his.

When they lifted me, the pull on my limbs was not as bad as I had expected. The main discomfort was the result of my body swinging this way and that as they walked: I was battered against the foliage and pricked by nettles and briars. The boys, our masters, carried us as though we were no more than featherweight. They didn't pay us any attention – we might as well have been dead meat.

I could see Leon, who was with me. Even with the weight he bore, he had a roll to his gait. I could still smell his urine, though it was dried on me by now. I hoped and hoped that he would fuck me soon.

Once out of the woods we were placed down at the deserted roadside. The Superiors sat on the grass and chatted, waiting, I supposed, for transport.

I caught only snatches of what they were saying for they kept their voices low. One spoke of Illyria, that land I had so often heard about. He had been there recently and told of the naked men who were put out for sale in the market and in the small shops which had opened up around it. The others called him Morgan.

'You can buy anything there,' he said. 'It's not like Tarne where all the Superiors have to be dark and the slaves must be fair. They would sell men like us just as readily. And you can try them before you buy. Fuck them there and then without paying anything.'

'What's the good of buying, then?' one of them laughed. 'You might as well just go to the market every day and try out the merchandise. You could work your way through the entire stock.'

'True,' his companion considered. 'I've never before had a boy who looks like a Superior. There was one there about my age and build. He was very beautiful and, in Tarne, he would easily have made the rank of Special Superior. Yet there he was, naked and available for anybody who fancied his arse. I fucked him with about five other citizens watching and cheering away. When I had done he was taken by each of them in turn. I'm not given to sympathy, but I did feel sorry for him. He'd probably been a slave there since he was a child. They treat them well as children I am told – they wait for them to become adult before they make them serve. I would have bought him if I'd had the money.'

'What would you have done with him?' asked another. 'He couldn't be a slave in Tarne if he looked as you say. It's against the rules. He would have to have been set free, and what's the use of that?'

So I found out one thing about this community. I had been picked by Caspar because I was fair. André was fair. Did this mean if I had different looks, I would have been offered a position as a Superior?

I kept wondering why Caspar didn't himself live in Tarne. Why did he only visit? Had he been disgraced in some way? Or was it a closed order which only a privileged few could join?

André was very close to me. The two poles had been placed together so we were forced to lie on our sides facing each other. Still he looked at me with those large, sad eyes. I reached across with my finger and stroked the back of his hand: I couldn't reach to do any more. He accepted this gesture silently. Attractive though he was, he wasn't for me. I was a slave like him and I told myself to concentrate my hopes on Leon, who could master me as I needed. Any other form of lovemaking seemed pale and worthless by comparison. I had to be dominated.

I remembered Troy, and Caspar's words on that first occasion when he had taken my body. Yes, he was right, there was something of the voyeur in me: I would have liked Troy to be bound there with us and to see him suffer as I had done. No part of me wanted to switch over and be one of the Superiors. I had found my place and I had Caspar to thank for it.

A cart came to collect us. Yet another dark-haired youth steered the horses. He was greeted by his compatriots with cheerful hellos. The back of the vehicle was open, covered in rough sacking. André and I were bundled in and covered away from prying eyes. Soon we were on our way.

'How long have you been at Tarne?' I whispered in the darkness beneath our covering.

I could feel André's warm breath on my chest and was able

to make contact with his skin. He didn't respond, and when I spoke he hushed me.

'It would not be wise for me to tell you more than I have already. You must be patient and time will answer your questions.'

I said nothing after that. Not long after, the cart ground to a halt and we heard gates being opened. We had arrived.

Once inside the courtyard, we were unloaded and carried towards the large, gloomy house which was all the more foreboding because of the evening mists swirling about it and beyond.

We were not taken, as I had expected, to some dungeon or left in a dark room. Instead we were deposited on the floor in a huge, opulent bedchamber. The four-poster that dominated the room was covered in red and black silk and had heavy velvet curtains around it. There were beautifully woven rugs placed here and there, underneath which was a deep-pile carpet. The polished wood underneath all this was displayed only where the boards met the hand-painted walls. Exquisite and detailed frescos depicted scenes of eastern boys in various states of bondage, many of them being fucked or made to suck older, less attractive men. They seemed to be in a sequence, starting at the door and going around the room. First a group of the lads were shown drinking and enjoying each other's company; then, in the next picture, they had been surprised by the older men who bore down on them with swords, their lustful expressions foretelling what was to happen. By the time the viewer reached the corner where a jug and basin stood ready for the occupant of the room to wash himself, the boys had been divested of their skimpy tunics and were being bound with ropes by the brutes who had captured them. They were then forced to suck cock: each of their captors had a huge member out of all proportion to the rest of his body. The expressions on the boys' faces were not, however, of fear or misery – they were of pure delight. Next, their arses were shown in detail, with hands prodding and examining. Then they were kneeling, offering their insides to the phallic monsters on which they were soon to be impaled. A whole wall was was dedicated to this and I couldn't even glance at it without being aware of my own cock pulsating away.

We had been freed from the indignity of being strung up to the two poles, and had been left on the floor where we had been untied. I tried to get up but was warned against the attempt by André.

'Stay where you are,' he said. 'They won't leave us here alone for long.'

'This is not where we are to be kept, surely,' I whispered. 'This isn't a room for slaves.'

André nodded over to the wall that faced the bed. I had presumed this to be a window for its entire length was curtained with black velvet drapes.

'We are to be put in there. One of the others was brought here months ago and he told me about it. Don't fear – this will be an easy way to begin your life here. Some have it much worse.'

Before I could speculate on what he meant, the door opened and Caspar stood before us. I had not expected him. Still less had I expected to see him dressed in a heavy purple dressing gown underneath which was an expensive and beautiful nightshirt. He was not the man I knew, who lived frugally and had never given any indication of wealth or a desire for such fripperies as now proved to be his.

He strode over to a bedside table and poured himself a drink. Then, crossing by us, he poked at us with his foot until we understood his instruction and knelt, facing the curtain. He pulled a cord. The drapes swished apart to reveal a caged adjunct to the room in which was a large bed and almost nothing else. The bed had sheets, blankets and pillows, but was not nearly as luscious as the one it faced. He unlocked the gate to the cage and pointed, showing us we were to go inside.

Once we were in, he turned the key again and lay back on his own bed, a drink in one hand. With the other, he was slowly undoing the buttons on his nightshirt to reveal his naked body and his slowly rising prick. He propped himself up on his pillows and sipped away – waiting.

We climbed on to the bed. Instinctively I reached for André's hand. We knelt there clutching each other's hands like two children afraid of what is to happen but excited by the prospect of it. For a long time nobody spoke a word. Caspar seemed to be enjoying our nervousness. He kept smiling at us, not at all in a friendly way. He may have been waiting for us to do something but we had no idea what was required of us. His cock was still half flaccid – he stroked it lovingly, sometimes letting his hand meander over his naked chest. His body, which was so familiar to me, looked more inviting in these surroundings. His chest hair seemed blacker, his pectorals more defined. The expensive clothing, carelessly pulled apart and cascading over the fine sheets on which he lay, accentuated the sexuality of the human form it had covered.

'Don't you poor slaves know what you are to do?' he said at last. Even his voice seemed different. It held more of a threat. His tone was mocking, heavy with sarcasm. 'I would have thought it was obvious, but maybe I'm overestimating your intelligence. Let's see if you can guess.'

André spoke. He lowered his head first, not daring to let it seem as though he had the right to enter into a conversation with one whose status was so far above his own.

'Are you going to use us, sir? Perhaps Master wants our arses closer to the bars so he can enter us.'

'I was right: you *are* stupid. Do you suppose I am too? If I wanted to fuck you, I wouldn't have put iron bars in the way of it. Pascal, you're at least able to find a small part of your brain which still works. You tell your asinine friend what he is to do.'

I lowered my head to match André's. I was trembling but

just about managing not to show it. When I spoke I could hear my voice shaking. I don't think this was because of fear. My nerves were tight from sexual anticipation. I needed to abandon myself to hedonism, to give my body to another man so he could swamp my brain with the joys of passion.

'Master, I think you wish to pleasure yourself. We are to try to entertain you by fucking each other so you have something to watch. We're to be used as animals are and must do in front of you what other men do privately.'

I had said the right thing. He leapt off the bed and stood very close to our cage, his cock almost inside it. He pressed closer still towards us, his hands gripping two of the bars at head height, and whispered very quietly.

'You have it, little slave boy. I don't care what you do, but if it doesn't make me come while I watch it, you will both be taken from here and scourged until you scream for mercy. Remember, your filthy bodies are only here to arouse me. I need to see clearly every part of your flesh. Moreover, I don't care if you hurt each other in the attempt. I'm not stimulated by sloppy romance. You're animals all right, so let me see you behave like it.'

He went swiftly back to his vantage point on the bed and we slowly raised our heads to look at each other.

André tentatively reached over to my shoulder and placed his hand on the nape of my neck. He stroked me briefly and then pushed – at first gently, but then more insistently. I let the pressure force me down until I had my face directly over his sweating groin. He pressed me into it and I let my tongue meet his skin. His prick was hot and it smelt strongly of sex. The wet head leaked on to my lips and I tried to clean it, thereby encouraging more and more of the oozing cream to cover my face. I took care not to hide what I did from our master, leaning my head towards the back wall of the cage so he could see my face and André's genitals. I licked carefully upward until the bloated head was at my lips. It entered easily, though the sides of my mouth soon ached with the effort of sucking it. I tasted his fluids deep inside my throat. They stung my tonsils as I swallowed. The more I sucked, the more I tasted his sap – an intense burning amid the other, less pungent flavour of his sweat.

Then I took the initiative and pushed him gently over on his back. I pulled him round so his arsehole was not hidden from Caspar. He raised his legs in the air and brought his hands round to pull aside his buttocks. His sphincter was thus displayed totally, robbing him of any humanity, denigrating him to being a mere fuckthing – a piece of meat.

I had to take myself as low as he was. I had to make that shithole something that was worth more than my entire body. I wanted to demonstrate to Caspar that this part of André, which most would recoil from, was, for me, to be worshipped. I licked it lovingly, wetting the hairs around it first and then pushing inside it with my tongue. It tasted bitter and my taste buds tingled where they met his secretions. I realised I was blocking our master's view with my body so I presumed to let my own shithole be an offering for him to enjoy. I mimicked André's action, pulling my arse wide so Caspar could see the place where I hoped I would soon be fucked by the golden-haired Adonis I was servicing.

'Stop,' Caspar shouted suddenly. 'Come to the front of the bars, my two animals.'

We did as ordered. By now we were past foreplay. We yearned either for release, or for a more acute stimulation to bring us to it. I could picture it in my head, but there was no ready means of its happening: I wanted a whip across my back.

Caspar approached us again. He was masturbating the whole time, his hand going up and down his member, firm and tight, building to his climax.

He stood near us, slowing his stroke and visibly calming for a moment or two. He dug into his pocket and tossed a sheath into the cage.

'One of you must fuck the other,' he said.

I dared to speak. It didn't matter – I was asking to be whipped: he couldn't do anything worse than deny me the pain I actively craved.

'Please, Master. I want you to have more pleasure yet. Would you like to see this slave punish me as you used to do yourself? If you'd be gracious enough to give him a whip, I will bend my back so he can flog me as you know I deserve.'

Caspar smiled again. I could tell that he was struggling between this attractive proposition and a desire to make me suffer mentally by refusing me. I was fortunate: he gave in to my wishes.

The whip he handed through the bars comprised many tails of twisted leather with a good, thick handle at its base. André took it uncertainly. He was looking towards me, trying, I supposed, to warn me he would not be able to hold back. He would have to hurt me for real.

I nodded to show I understood his concerns and they were of no matter. I knelt on the floor by the edge of the bed and bent my torso over the mattress with my arms spread over it, away from my body. I put my head down and waited. André must have been standing to the side of me: the first swipe fell from that direction.

Pain is better than gentle pleasure. Where the loving touch of a man allows the body to grow slowly towards its fulfilment, the cut of a lash immediately takes one even beyond orgasm. It cracks across the skin like fire and there can be no further place for the senses to take you. The multi-tailed lash that scourged me gave me this sensation many times over with the first swipe. I clamoured for more and was rewarded with another ferocious hail of stings.

The very sound of the tails, swishing through the air as they fell on my naked skin, was making me reel. I bawled loudly – a bestial shout of pain and pleasure. I couldn't bear for this to end.

Caspar allowed me to be flogged until I was nearly spent. Then he told André to cease and instructed him to screw my arse.

André pulled me off the bed. I was forgetting myself and had expected to be fucked where I was. André was still aware we were on show. Taking me in my former position would have afforded our master a restricted view. Instead André forced me to place myself on all fours facing the bars. He entered me slowly, pushing, little by little, up my anal passage so it yielded to his cock by degrees. My back was too painful for him to approach. Maybe he knew this or maybe he was still mindful of the command to remain displayed at all times. He supported himself against my buttocks with his hands, and half bent his knees to give his thrust more power. I was able to sneak a glance at Caspar, who was keeping the strokes on his cock in time with the shoves of André's groin against my backside. André grabbed my penis with one hand and tried to wank me, but he couldn't manage it and I took over myself.

He came before I did. The slaps of his body against mine slowed and then culminated in five long pushes which brought his come out of him. He had been holding his breath, but now he let it out in a low gasp.

I looked to Caspar, afraid he would be angry André had come without asking, but he was beyond caring. He was very near to coming himself and so I attended to my own cock in order to escape the dreadful prospect of being chained up again before I could release my spunk.

I think we both reached our orgasm at the same time, but I could only tell from the shout Caspar gave which coincided with a rush of come splashing out of my piss-slit and over the floor in front of me. I fell into it like a puppet whose strings have been cut all at once. I lay where I was, not moving. Caspar must have drawn the curtains across soon afterwards. Blackness eventually descended over my brain and, presently, I began to dream.

Three

Denton awoke. The grudging dawn had spread its greyness into the room where they lay. He had not slept well – and he had no great rush to rise and decide what he should do about the task that had been entrusted to him. The boy, Cuthwin, lay still and peaceful, his arms still tightly around Denton. His long eyelashes flickered as he dreamt. He had been talking in his sleep – that must have been what had brought Denton out of his own fitful slumber. Cuthwin murmured still – though what he said was not discernible. Denton felt ashamed of himself for having submitted to the activities of the night before. He felt a need to dress in his most puritanical suit of clothes and go and have a man-to-man conversation with the landlord on as masculine a subject as he could think of – the techniques of battle perhaps. At least that was what his brain told him to do. His heart wanted different, and his cock agreed with his heart. He had promised to fuck this delicate young thing when the morning arrived. Now it was nearly time. He could wake him by shoving his already hard cock up that pretty little arse.

Cuthwin nuzzled closer to him and gabbled something. It

sounded as though he was having a bad dream. Denton's protective side overcame his bestial impulses and he cuddled Cuthwin tightly until he calmed and his breath became even and deep once more.

It was not more than half an hour later that Morgan appeared. He was already dressed and didn't seem to have the least trace of a hangover. Denton could tell from his unannounced entrance and the scowl he wore on his face that he wasn't making a friendly or a social call.

'You have my property still,' he said. 'I want it back.'

It didn't at first occur to Denton that Morgan was talking about the slave and not some bauble which had been handed over the previous evening and forgotten about. He was about to say he didn't remember having been given any such thing, when Morgan yanked Cuthwin out of his sleep and out of the bed.

Cuthwin went white and stood naked and trembling before his master. The shivering might have been caused by the coldness of the room, but the look of horror he wore appeared to take no account of his obvious excuse. He had, after all, had very little choice in where he slept and had been given to Denton by the very man who was now behaving like a jealous husband.

Morgan announced brusquely that it was time to get going. Cuthwin was to be ready for him in the yard within ten minutes or he would have his arse whipped as it had never been whipped before.

Denton protested. Morgan had every right to treat Cuthwin badly – though it seemed unfair and unnecessary – but he, Denton, had been given the slave for the night and it wasn't good manners to take him back as though their sleeping together had been a clandestine affair discovered too late to prevent its happening.

He was surprised to notice Cuthwin frantically signing to him to hold his peace and not make trouble. No doubt this was because it would be he, not Denton, who would suffer for it. Denton let his words tail off into nothing.

Morgan looked at him scornfully. Beautiful though he was, his personality showed through and marred the youthful symmetry of his face. He could look downright unpleasant and captivatingly handsome at the same time. With a cursory nod at Denton, he was gone. Cuthwin came over to the bed and grasped Denton's hand.

'I have to go back, but you will come and find me? I'm to be taken away soon and I'm afraid. You're the first person who I've been able to tell who can help me. Will you find me?'

'You're at the community. I know where you are, but what can I do?'

Denton was worried by the fear in the lad's voice. He had been led to believe they'd all agreed to enter into this lifestyle. Surely there was no reason to mistreat men who delighted in being abused.

'My master, Morgan, he threatens to take me to Illyria and sell me on the market there. You could – you could buy me and take me away. Please, I like you so much and you like me just a little, don't you?'

His language was stilted, or perhaps it had the trace of a foreign accent about it. His plea was the first hint of something more sinister than orgiastic indulgence going on at the community.

'You see,' said Denton's bad angel. 'Perhaps last night's pleasure had been mixed in with the work you have to do after all.'

I don't think Matilda would see it that way, Dention thought to himself. His wife liked all men to have eyes only for her. She couldn't abide the thought of males who had no interest, not only in her own charms, but in female bodies generally. They were, she maintained, insane: all men who were unavailable to her were labelled insane.

93

'I thought you had agreed to what happens in that house. I thought you wanted it.'

'I was a slave in Illyria long before I came to Tarne,' Cuthwin said. 'I was sold to a man who, though he doesn't live in the community, brings us our newcomers. He encourages some; some ask; some are tricked and some forced. I was bought by him – I had no choice. Then I was given to Morgan as his special slave, but he's tired of me and wants a change. Either I'll be sold or . . .'

'Or what?' Denton asked. The boy was giving quick nervous glances over his shoulder, terrified Morgan might return and catch him.

'Or I'll be killed,' he said.

Later, at breakfast, the landlord had given Denton a knowing wink and asked slyly if he had slept well. Denton felt embarrassed at having given into his latent homosexuality and worried about what he had been told by the slave. He purported to have fallen asleep as soon as he had climbed into bed. He had, he said, slept soundly and had not stirred until morning.

The landlord was too good a businessman to argue with this fabrication, but he retained the arch look. It was absolutely clear he knew what had transpired.

'You'll stay with us until you find your son, I hope?' he asked. 'There's nowhere else to go, I can assure you of that.'

Denton agreed and laid down a bag of coins, telling his host to let him know when it had been spent. He was worried. This mission had begun as a typical case of youthful rebellion: all he had to do was find the whereabouts of this Troy and tell his parents where he was. Now it transpired that he, Denton, might be becoming involved in slavery for profit and murder. Not only this, but he had bedded one of the potential victims who was now looking exclusively to him for help. What made the lad fear for his life? Had others been killed and had Cuthwin known about it?

Denied the fuck he had expected, Denton felt an urgent need to strip off his clothing and attend to the erection that pressed against his thigh. His head swam with thoughts of others from the community coming into the tavern and the chance of repeating the scenes he had experienced. The urge was too great to resist – he had to come right away or he would burst. He pushed his empty plate aside and went back to his room.

He lay on the bed, which still had the impression Cuthwin had left there beside Denton. Hugging the pillow as if it was a living thing, he rolled over and let his thoughts meander.

Cuthwin was a slave – that fact nagged at him. What was it that seemed so important about this? He had known Cuthwin was a slave: he had demonstrated it in the tavern and in the bedroom.

No, it was that Cuthwin had, at least at first, been an unwilling slave. He had been captured and taken to Illyria and there sold on the market like an animal.

He should have abhorred this idea. It should have been something horrible to contemplate. After all, it wasn't right men should be sold against their will. The life they were forced to lead afterwards was anathema to Denton – or at least it had been.

He forced himself to picture women in his mind and to imagine them taking off their clothes for his delectation. That should put everything into perspective, shouldn't it?

Curiously, the flights of fancy he conjured refused to stick to the gender he had given them. They began as beautiful females and each removed her clothing willingly to expose not the naked breasts and vagina to make Denton feel normal again, but the smooth, muscled chest and the long thin penis he had seen on the slave. When he focused once more on their faces,

95

each one had turned into Cuthwin and each one beckoned to him whispering, calling:

'I was a slave in Illyria . . . I was sold to a man . . . Some are tricked and some forced . . . I had no choice . . . Either I'll be sold or . . . Or I'll be killed . . .'

Then another man entered Denton's dream. It was not a person he knew and not one he was aware of even having seen before. His skin was white and his hair black. He had sharp, blue eyes which pierced right through and into Denton's very soul. His body was hairy from his strong legs to the top of his sculptured chest. He had thick, powerful arms and he was dressed in a snow-white shirt which covered little, for it was open and loose. His trousers were similar to the ones Morgan had worn: they were old-fashioned, buckled where they finished just below the knee. He was younger than Denton but had the air of someone with authority who deferred to no one. His arms were extended towards Denton, tempting him into them where he might lose himself for ever.

Denton shook himself out of this reverie and the phantom vanished. For some reason, it had frightened him. He told himself it was merely his own guilt that disturbed him. He was sinking further and further into his true nature and his conscious mind was battling against it, trying to pull him back into being that cold, miserable wage-earner his life demanded he be.

He shut his eyes and deliberately brought the ghost back into his mind. The spectre reappeared, this time with Cuthwin kneeling at his feet. Cuthwin was trying to tell Denton something.

'This is the man who bought me . . .'

The voice was as audible to him as though Cuthwin had spoken out loud. It was urgent and full of import.

'This is the man who bought me . . .'

Again . . . Denton reached down to his belt and undid it. In

96

a few seconds he had pulled his shirt open and ripped his trousers apart to free his sex. His hands (if they were still his own – they felt to him like another's) ran over his body and down – down to his cock, under his balls, stroking and caressing.

Trying hard to concentrate on the form in his mind, he rubbed the head of his penis. The man he had conjured smiled encouragingly.

'Yes,' he seemed to say. 'Wank yourself in front of my beautiful body. Enjoy what you see. Let this maleness bring you to your fulfilment. Look at my handsome face, into my eyes. You can't escape it. You can't deny that you want it . . .'

Denton abandoned himself to it and wanked. As he rubbed his sex, additional thoughts came to him to deepen the pool of lust into which he was sinking. His hands were linked by chains. He wore a collar around his neck, just like the slave who still knelt at the feet of the ghost.

Then he was no longer in his room at the inn. He was on some platform and many others were around him. He was being sold, he was being made to wank, not for himself but for the amusement of many others. The body he had previously called his own was his no longer.

He sat up quickly and stripped off his shirt. His naked back was instantly covered in imaginary welts. He had been scourged and would be flogged again before long. He didn't leave off wanking – it was right he should be whipped.

'I'm just a slave,' he said out loud. 'I need to be punished by my masters. Come to me and take me. I want to be owned by you.'

The phantom smiled at him as if to tell him it was already so. The words came tumbling out of Denton's mouth as his semen boiled upward and erupted. He panted, gasped and finally shouted in anguish. It was over. He had come.

★　★　★

The pictures vanished from his mind. He felt dirty and ashamed. This turnabout was not unusual for him. He was aware enough of the workings of the mind to know it was a counter-reaction to having let his true self off the leash to run freely over the straitjacketed, frigid personality he had taken to in his everyday life.

He usually came back to himself after having a long bath, cleaning his body and his mind of the sinful thoughts that had overtaken it. He regarded these incidents as aberrations, not really him, not to be taken seriously.

This time it was different. He had touched on something that cut through his armour of indifference and made him realise he was a man with sexual urges which would never completely go away. He could feel his shameful inner self leaking out from the shell he had created round it. He could no longer keep it in.

Who was the man he had seen? How could he appear so clearly – someone he had never met? He wasn't the type Denton would usually fantasise about. Why had he heard Cuthwin telling him what he had?

One thing was certain: he had to do something about the slave. He would never be able to live in peace, with his good angel forever reproaching him, forever telling him he had abandoned a boy who had put all trust in him.

Caspar snuffed out the candle and quietly sat back on the satin-draped throne. He was still smiling.

In front of him, surrounded by chalked lines and circles, Cuthwin lay spread-eagled. He was naked. His arms and legs were tied to pegs which stretched his body as far wide as it could go. His eyes still glanced around wildly, but his prick was now soft and seeping come.

Also in the room, Morgan: facing Caspar from across the floor. He had a knife in his hands, blood still dripping from it.

A large fowl lay at his feet, its neck severed. It jerked twice and then lay still.

'You've done well finding this Denton for us,' Caspar said to Morgan. 'I knew some stranger would come snooping around before long.'

He looked at Cuthwin's vulnerable body and for a moment seemed as though he might have used it. Cuthwin's penis began to grow again and Morgan scoffed.

'I think our filthy little slave here hasn't had enough of the stranger's cock. Look at him. We only have to mention the man's existence and he gets hard. It's barely a minute since I wanked him and allowed his spunk to splash over his belly. Now he wants it again. Should I thrash him or fuck him? I can't make up my mind which. It's such a difficult decision.'

Caspar wasn't listening. His mind was far away, remembering things he had read when he was only a youngster. Could it be true? Could it be possible his great-grandfather had been able to see events that had not yet happened? This stranger's presence had been predicted. It followed that the other writings must also be accurate.

'How can you be sure he's dangerous?' Morgan asked gruffly.

'If what you say is right, he won't be.' Caspar replied. 'And, to answer your other question, you must leave this slave alone for a while. He finds this infiltrator attractive. So be it. Maybe the stranger returns the compliment. Cuthwin can be our bait.'

'What should I do?' Morgan growled. 'Chain him to a rock at the crossroads and wait for this Denton to pass by?'

He wiped the fowl's blood from the knife with a cloth and cast it aside. He stood over the prostrate boy on the floor and spat on to his face.

'He's pretty enough,' he went on. 'But, if I were Denton, I wouldn't risk anything to save him. After all, he's only a slave. There are plenty more where he came from.'

'You don't understand ordinary people, do you?' Caspar

sneered. 'They have all sorts of misguided ideas of goodness and morality. Denton won't see him as a mere slave. He'll see him as a lad who's become his friend, perhaps more than a friend. He'll be duty-bound to do whatever he can for him. All we have to do is to persuade him that our little beauty is in real peril. Do you think you could manage that?'

Morgan looked down at Cuthwin, who was trembling from head to foot. Morgan grinned, his face creasing into an expression of pure malice.

'Look at him,' he said to Caspar. '*He* knows I can put him in real peril, even if you don't. I shall relish the task. Perhaps I might involve some of those untamed drunkards from the village. They're all bullies, brimming over with their manliness. It would be like throwing a little lamb to a pack of wolves.'

Caspar closed his eyes as though suddenly pained by too much conversation.

'You don't have to tell me the details. Just let me know when you have the stranger in chains and locked in one of my dungeons. Then everything will be safe.'

'You can trust me,' Morgan said. 'I'm not like Leon, even though you give him more responsibility than you give me. He's weak. I don't know why you bother with him. Unless you fancy his arse.'

Caspar suddenly exploded with rage. 'I'm not some whore who will give my body to another Superior! When I fuck, I'm on top and if you think otherwise you'll feel my whip across your back, you bastard!'

Morgan was surprised by the vehemence of his anger, but stood his ground.

'I just think you give Leon too much. He's still relatively new here. I meant no offence.'

Caspar changed to a more conciliatory tone, leaning forward as he spoke.

'You are more than Leon. Leon is content to have a pretty arse to stick his cock into.' He paused for a moment, considering whether it would be wise to say more. 'The boy, Pascal, who I've given to Leon to screw whenever he wants to, is someone I took a fancy to, nothing more.'

Morgan had to content himself with this for Caspar was not going to say anything further and he knew it. Morgan wished he didn't feel as though he was being cheated all the time. It was true: he had been given responsibility and a position of power over most of the other Superiors. He had been given his own personal slave and he could take his pick of the others whenever he wanted, but he was envious and scathing towards Leon.

He undid his trousers and brought his cock out. It was flaccid because of the drink he had taken the night before. He scratched his stomach as he let go of the contents of his bladder. The hot piss washed over Cuthwin, taking the come with it and forming puddles by the side of his body. Cuthwin arched his back, accepting the urine and even seeming to encourage it.

'Filthy little pig,' his master said. 'Take my piss, you piece of shit. When I get hard again, I'll find some village boy's spunk to add to it. Till then you'll stay here and think about the man who will come to attempt to rescue you. You will be the bait in our trap. When we've finished with him, we'll decide whether to sell you or keep you.'

He directed the jet across the boy's face. Cuthwin opened his mouth and Morgan pissed directly down his throat. Cuthwin drank as much as he was able, but was soon coughing and spluttering as more and more salty liquid splashed over his lips, flooded his eyes and drenched his hair.

Morgan finished.

'You can lie there in it till I come for you again.' He addressed Caspar. 'I need more sleep. Is it permitted for me to go?'

Caspar nodded. 'I have things to do. I must be out of here before noon. You've done well. I'm pleased.'

101

Morgan left and very shortly afterwards Caspar followed him. Cuthwin was left in the dark, his penis slowly growing at the thought of his master's return.

The landlord wiped his hands on his apron and went back to cleaning the tables.

'What you say is serious,' he said. 'But I don't see what we can do about it. If they are buying slaves, it isn't illegal. If a man is property in Illyria, he remains so here until such time as the Elders decide to alter the law. I can't see them ever doing that. It would cause too much discontent among the very people who they fear the most. They might have a mandate to govern, but they know they're treading a tightrope. A rising amongst those who still want us to be under Illyria's rule would be the last thing they'll want to encourage.'

Denton knew he spoke the truth but he wasn't satisfied. Illyria had been a wanton place, even in the days of his own childhood. It was without moral strictures and was thought of as barbaric in the way its people treated those over whom they had power, but it had never been evil.

He had not told the landlord about the vision that had come to him. It had been all he could do to confess to having slept with Cuthwin and to reiterate what the boy had told him. He needed an ally. There was nobody else he could trust. Indeed, he wasn't entirely sure he could trust his host. For all he knew, the landlord could be one of them.

'We have to do something,' Denton said. 'Will you help me or won't you?'

'I run a tavern,' the other answered. 'I'm not brave and I'm not reckless. I have to look after myself. I will let you stay here for as long as you have to. I want you to find this Troy if you have to, and I even support what you say about the boy, Cuthwin, but I can't do anything because there's nothing I *can* do. I'm sure you understand.'

The room had become suddenly cold. Denton shuddered. The landlord looked up enquiringly.

'Somebody just walked over my grave,' Denton said.

At the same time, not far away, a cockerel was twitching its life away on the floor at the feet of the naked body of the boy whom Denton had resolved to help escape.

Pascal

André and I were allowed to sleep for most of the day. Caspar closed the curtains surrounding our cage and for a short while, as far as I could tell, fell asleep himself. Then we heard him get up and leave the room.

I held André close to me. He was breathing gently against my neck. His short beard tickled my skin. I buried my nose in his hair and took time to relish the wonderful smell of it. I couldn't stay awake and a number of hours must have passed, but when I did eventually come to, neither of us had moved at all.

I remembered Troy and wondered if it would have been like this with him. Would he have been as gently accepting of everything that came his way? André was no coward and he was certainly strong – nobody could accuse him of being less than masculine. However, he was not ashamed of being loved and he was just as ready to demonstrate the return of affection he felt. I wanted to ask him if he ever thought of freedom. It was possible he didn't want it. Maybe he was content – I hoped so.

He opened his eyes at last. The very first thing he did was

lock his lips on to mine. We might have been in the lap of luxury at that moment. I felt even more for him than I had done for Caspar, though perhaps 'more' is the wrong word. Perhaps 'different' would better describe it: it was a deeper, truer emotion. I knew Caspar represented little more than sex to me. He was exciting and dangerous, but he could never aspire to take the place in my heart that André had just made his own.

'They won't let us stay like this,' he said. His voice was calm, but it was resentful. He held my face in his hands and kissed my eyelids gently. 'I've been here for a long, long time. I always hoped somebody like you would one day come to me. Does that seem stupid?'

'No,' I replied. 'I feel it too. I thought I was immature. I thought I couldn't feel like this for another man, but, earlier – when we had to fuck for Caspar – it wasn't just the sex: I was at one with you. I knew it then, and I know it now.' I stopped, embarrassed, but he kissed me again to encourage me to speak further. 'André, let's make a bond between us now. Let's say we'll be together, no matter what happens.'

'Tarne doesn't allow it,' he said shortly and bitterly.

'Then let's leave Tarne. We could go. Surely they won't prevent us. I could ask Caspar. He's been my friend and he persuaded me to come here. I'll say I've made a mistake.'

'You don't understand, do you?' he said. 'Caspar isn't going to let you go. It's part of some mad idea he has about preserving his youth. You've been lured here by sex. Now he has you in his menagerie, he won't release you back into the world. Still less would he let me go. This isn't a game he's playing. He believes in the Devil and he believes he is supreme over other men because of it. A farmer breeding pigs for slaughter has more care for his charges than Caspar does. He's evil.'

'You're wrong,' I said weakly. 'I know him. We've been friends for months.'

'You're not the first. There's something he said once about

105

some of us slaves, myself one of them, being useless to him because we were forced to come here: we, who were sold or captured. He said he had others to make his favourites. He picked out one young lad who, like you, had thought Caspar was his friend. He had been miserable here, but they hadn't allowed him to go back to his family. He was taken away from us and we never saw him again.'

'Then perhaps he did go back home.'

'No.' André shook his head sadly and definitely. 'Something terrible's happened to him. Don't ask me how I know it, I just do. One every year, sometimes taken from among his stock and sometimes brought in specially. It's always around the same time. I've heard whisperings about what happens but nobody really knows. I think you may be in very great danger. Be careful for yourself. I don't want anything to happen to you – I couldn't bear it.'

I knew in my gut he was speaking the truth, but I didn't want to accept it. I tried not to be frightened by what he said, tried to think calmly. I resolved to find a way to leave Tarne and, when I did, to take André with me.

The mansion was ancient and partly ruined. We were warm enough, for each area had a blazing fire to heat it and the walls were thick enough to keep out the chill that pervaded Tarne, even now, in late spring.

Stairs wound up the centre of the building. I supposed they led to the Superiors' sleeping quarters. There were kitchens at the back, where on my first day, as soon as Caspar had dismissed André and me, I had been set to work preparing vegetables. I was one of four who were given this job under the supervision of one of the older slaves who happened to have a talent for cooking. We were allowed to talk, but every time I asked about the community – how long were we to be kept here? what did the Superiors expect of us? – questions which I had expected to be answered on my first day, they clammed up and the cook changed the subject very obviously.

I'd presumed from what had happened that André and I were to remain Caspar's special interest. This was not the case and I was glad of it, for I was given to Leon. I thought, rightly as it happened, that he would be kind to me. When he first came for me, it made some sense of my purpose at Tarne. It was in the late evening of that first working day that he came to the kitchens and beckoned. I followed him into the corridor. He ran his hand over my body and I writhed under his touch.

'You are mine from now on,' he told me. 'I am able to mark you out as my property, though the others will have use of you. Tonight I intend to fuck your arse. You've experienced this before I take it?'

I nodded, swallowing the temptation to kiss his thick, dark lips. His chin was covered with the beginnings of a beard. I wanted to feel that stubble scratching against me. I wanted his tongue in my mouth, his prick up my arse.

'Caspar has told us a little about you,' Leon went on. 'It will be difficult for you at first, but your natural inclinations will teach how to learn obedience and behave in the way which is required of you. Follow me.'

His room was not, he explained, near to where the others slept. He was what they called a Special Superior and therefore had privileges that all but one of the others were denied.

His bed was big and roomy; at the foot of it was a small bunk which was welded to the floor. A leg iron was fastened to one of its supports. This was surely where I would be sleeping that night.

He undressed quickly. His body was every bit as good as Caspar's and, though his cock was not as big, it was shaped, where Caspar's was blunt. He climbed into bed and motioned for me to get in beside him. I did so and lay there, not sure of what I was meant to do.

'What did I say earlier?' he said. His tone was vexed and I panicked slightly. My mind raced over his previous words and I luckily hit on the right sentence.

'You said you were going to fuck me, sir.'

'Can I fuck your arse if you're lying on your back? Are you stupid?'

'I'm sorry, sir.'

I turned over on to my front. I watched him reach for a sheath and roll it over that, now hard, cock. His hand gripped under my stomach, lifting that part of me so that my buttocks were available to him. This was done in an impatient way, indicating I should have known and put myself in the position without his having to do it for me.

'You said you'd been fucked before. It doesn't seem like it from the way you place yourself. Each time I have cause to remind you in the future will result in five strokes from my lash. Do you understand?'

'Yes, sir.'

I didn't want him to be annoyed with me, I wanted him to smile again in the same crooked, quirky way he had when he pissed over me in the woods. His annoyance made me feel stupid and unworthy. I resolved to make myself the best fuck he'd had for a long time.

He pushed his cock into my anus slowly, savouring it. As the muscle gave way to the assault, I tensed and then forced myself to relax again. It hurt, but I could take it. I could take anything he wanted to give me.

I moved my buttocks to meet his thrust. Then I felt his pubic hair brushing against me. The area where our bodies met immediately produced sweat, a dribble of which ran down into the crack of my arse.

He brought his hands to my nipples and squeezed them painfully. I gritted my teeth and waited for the pain to ease. It did soon enough and, in its place, a warmth welled up in my breast. My nipples cried out for more. He gripped them again and pulled. As he did so, his lower body began to pump into me. I responded the best I could, pushing backward as he came towards me and pulling as he withdrew. I took care to tighten the muscles that gripped his penis. I didn't want him to think me too loose for his pleasure.

'That's better, little slave,' he groaned. 'I like that. I like that!'

He brought one of his palms to my mouth and, guessing this was what was required, I licked it like a dog. He let my saliva build up on his hand and then rubbed it over the rest of my face before returning for more.

My insides were full of him and my heart was his completely. Again, there was the desire to tell him this; again, I held my tongue.

Then the strokes of his lust quickened in pace and I knew he was near to coming. He let out a long, pained sigh and gave me three final pushes. Then he pulled his cock out of me.

'You want to come too, don't you?' he said.

'If it's allowed me, I would like to very much, sir.'

I was desperate for it. During most of my day's labour, my cock had not had more than a moment's peace. I spent hours thinking of being whipped; chained; hog-tied; pissed on; I told myself constantly I was now a slave as I had always wanted to be. Whenever I had thought about such things in the past, I had masturbated very soon afterwards, the images in my head serving as fuel for my cock's release.

'You're not to. I won't allow it.'

He fumbled under the bed and brought out a length of rope. My heart sank. I was to be tied up so I couldn't possibly touch myself. I would have to be patient through the night, chained at the foot of this beautiful man's bed with my hands unable to do what every part of my body demanded of them.

Sure enough, he forced my arms behind me and bound me

tightly. Then he pushed me off the bed. I lay on the floor where I had fallen, hurt and miserable.

'Get on to that slave cot,' he said.

I did so and he locked my ankle into the leg iron.

'I must sleep now. If you need to piss in the night, you must do it over yourself. If you do, you'll have to wash the bed coverings tomorrow.'

There was a long silence. Then he extinguished the light and I was left to lie there in the dark. Sleep was impossible, knowing, only a few feet away, was the man who I'd hoped would love me.

'Welcome to Tarne, slave. You'll be satisfactory before long and, when you are, I'll allow you to get rid of some of that spunk that's troubling you so much.'

He sounded kindly again. This was the same as I had so often had from Caspar: that mixture of kindness and cruelty. One moment he was the brother you always wanted and the next the bully you hated.

The trouble was, I didn't know which side of Caspar – or of Leon – I responded to. Perhaps a man can find a certain romance in being dominated.

I had not pissed myself in the night and so was spared having to wash the sheets. Leon let me piss in the yard and there I saw other slaves, each with a master assigned to him, relieving themselves as I was doing. I was taken back indoors and once more set to my tasks in the kitchens.

When I was not with Leon, I was told I would sleep with the other slaves, next to André. I didn't know then which of these two men, Leon and André, I desired the more. Love must come unbidden into our lives. I was trying to force it and was rewarded with confusion.

During those nights when our special masters did not require us, we slaves were kept in cages on the lower floor. We were allowed blankets, but our upper bodies were usually unclothed. Our ankles were chained one to another, the large iron links eventually leading to rivets in the stone wall at the back of our prison.

There were about six of us in the pen where I was to spend the majority of my resting hours. Most of them were about my age, but there were a couple who were older and to whom I would learn to defer when they suggested we be quiet and sleep or, as sometimes would happen, when they wanted to copy their masters' behaviour and take our arses or our mouths for their own pleasure.

My work in the kitchens had not been arduous, but, despite the trousers I had been given to wear, I had still thought about nothing but sex. Cook had noticed my erection and he'd smiled knowingly, but had said nothing.

I had been good and not touched myself. I lay back and pulled the prickly woollen covering over me. Our masters dressed us in knee-breeches, ragged and torn, but a covering of some sort and one for which I was grateful. I had taken these off and was naked for the first time that day. The temptation to touch my cock was overwhelming but I dared not do it.

I was the only one who had been shaved and I was ashamed of it. I didn't know why. For all I could tell, it was something each and every one of them had had to go through. Eventually, I would be allowed back my body hair, though that on my head, like the others', would still be cropped regularly.

André, next to me, came up very close and took me in his arms. I was ridiculously grateful for this demonstration of his love and I hugged him back urgently. I was crying quietly, not from self-pity, but from gratitude that anyone in this place should show me tenderness and love. I wanted to be abused, yes, but I also needed to feel a man's protective arms around me and to know I was still capable of receiving a gentle caress.

'Hush now,' he said. 'Hush! It's all right. I know how difficult it is at first. You'll get used to it. It is only Caspar and Morgan you have to fear. Most of the others are not monsters. They're just strict. Leon will teach you. He will not punish you unfairly.'

'I know,' I cried. 'It's just that . . .'

'We are allowed to do as we wish once they have left us here,' André said. 'This is our time. As long as we can still be hard for them when they want us, then we shall not suffer for it.'

'What if Leon wants me in the night?'

'He won't. As I said, he's not wicked like the other two. It's very rare that we're sent for once we've been caged for the night. Let me make love to you.'

I heard others in the cage moving about in the darkness. The chains tugged at my legs as they were dragged over the floor. However, there was enough length to allow us to couple with each other. I pulled André on top of me and opened my legs for him.

He bent down and sucked my cock into his mouth. It was like the first time it had ever happened. I experienced the soaring feeling of relief as he mouthed up and down and I gripped his head in my hands, his hair trailing through my fingers.

He let it go for a second and pushed up towards my mouth. His tongue and mine entwined passionately. I explored the inside of his mouth with a fervour born of long frustration. My hands reached down and gripped the flesh of his buttocks. I scratched hard. He kissed me all the more as I continued to mark his skin up the sides of his chest and along his biceps.

'When I first saw you, in the wood, I wanted Caspar to allow us to do this,' he said. 'I was being punished that day. One of their favourite chastisements is to put you in front of sex and not let you come. I haven't done since we were made to fuck for Caspar. Have you?'

I shook my head and grunted a denial. I was busily kissing his eyelids, his brows, his nose.

'He even had you shaved because he knows I like to see that. It's one of the things I can't help myself with. I find you so wonderful looking as you do.'

'Don't talk,' I said hoarsely. 'Fuck me.'

'That I can't do. It isn't allowed. Unless we do it this way –'

He pushed his finger into my anus and felt around the hot inside of my passage. Then he inserted another and another. He pushed up and down. He gave me a last kiss on the lips and returned his mouth to my penis.

His finger-fucking and the tight suction on my cock was sheer ecstasy. I felt a rush coming up my sex from deep inside of me. It built rapidly into a burning need for release and I gratefully filled his mouth with my seed.

He took it inside him and then brought his face on to my chest. He dribbled the come from his lips all over me, his hand now pumping away at his own cock. In seconds he was thrusting his body about with the strain of his oncoming orgasm. I heard others around sigh as, one by one, they spurted over each other.

André's come hit me in the face and splattered over me to mingle with my own juices on my chest. He grabbed me again and we kissed as we had before.

Then we fell asleep. Two slaves, chained to others and covered in the thick white cream of our pent-up lust.

Four

For two nights Denton stayed at the inn wondering what to do. The two boys did not reappear as he only half hoped they might. Had they done, he would have had to galvanise himself into some sort of action. He had gone over in his head what he might do. Confront Morgan? That would surely be a bad idea. He would deny everything, or he might well admit it and challenge Denton to do something. Whatever followed would surely result in nothing more than Cuthwin's being punished for having talked to him in the first place, or worse. Denton next considered trying to befriend Morgan: playing undercover. Would it be possible to secure an invitation to the mansion and thereby find out what was going on? What he would do once he had this knowledge he had no idea at all. He wasn't the type to practise any heroics, but at least he would know what he was dealing with.

This was more or less what he had decided to do, but he didn't relish it. Morgan was not going to be the easiest person to allow his trust to be gained. Also, he, Denton, had already put himself in a subservient position to the brute. He had, he admitted, been indiscreet and had compromised his investigations by succumbing to sexual temptation. The only way forward would be to go further down that path: to ask for more.

The prospect was repulsive to his good angel and extremely attractive to his bad one. He appeased the former by persuading himself he had no choice in the matter. He was, he thought grandiloquently, sacrificing his personal morality for the greater good of others. Had he examined his heart, he would have been less sure of his motives. The rescue of Cuthwin, the discovery of the boy whose disappearance had brought him there, the financial demands of his nagging wife, and even his professional respect were nothing to wanting to further explore the dark depths of his desire for submission.

So, true to his usual quiescence, he sat and waited for something to happen. Every morning he walked up the miserable road that led to the manor. He stopped by the edge of the high wall that surrounded the building, not daring to go further where he might be seen. He didn't know what he hoped for. Had anybody gone in or out, he would not have had the slightest idea what he might say to them. Had he seen Morgan, he had no excuse ready for his presence there and would probably have hidden until the coast was clear again.

There was something that both attracted and repelled beyond those ornate gates. If only he could see what lay beyond without risking becoming part of it. He remembered his dream and the man who had appeared to him. Though he tried to find the idea preposterous, he knew deep down that what he had seen was more than the conjurings of his sex-infested subconscious. The phantom visitor, like the mysterious place from which he had surely come, had appalled and intrigued. The magician's cave was within Denton's reach and the Evil One beckoned him into it. Denton was fighting the spell the best he could, but he knew he would soon have to obey.

The landlord of the inn didn't speak about the mansion any more. He was polite to his guest, but not nearly as open as he had been. He seemed to regard Denton as a dangerous fool: tampering with things he knew nothing about and surely on a course for disaster. Denton was surprised, therefore, to arrive back from his morning walk to find his host waiting for him expectantly – there was news.

'You've had a visitor,' he said before Denton had managed to get through the door. 'I told you to keep away from these people, but you wouldn't listen. Morgan has been asking for you.'

'That's impossible,' the other replied. 'I would have seen him on the road. Nobody passed me.'

'You can't be that innocent, surely! He knows where you go each morning. He's watched you. In fact, he seems to find your methods of investigation a source of great amusement. He can hide himself from your snooping without any difficulty. They don't have to use the main road to reach the village if they don't want to.'

The landlord sat down and considered for a moment. Denton waited. The man's attitude suggested he was deciding whether or not to say what was in his mind. Presently, he reached for Denton's arm and firmly pulled him to the seat opposite. Once he was sure his words were to be afforded their full importance he leant in close and said, 'I advise you to go home, my friend. I know you have money to earn but there are safer ways of doing it. You'd be safer risking a bloody nose by discovering an adulterous husband fucking his mistress. You'd even be better working for the Elders, spying on criminals. This community you seem so keen to reform is not merely a source of physical danger . . .'

He paused. There was more, but he was reluctant to say it. However, he had gone so far and could not hold back now. He gripped Denton's wrists as he spoke; his jaw was tight and he was finding it impossible to look his guest in the eyes.

'Do you know what happens to the souls of men who are given to devils?'

Denton laughed nervously, trying to appear as though the idea was absurd, but he was scared. He had suspected this all along. His phantom visitor, the strange aura the house emitted, even his own change of character – it had to have something to do with the supernatural. Denton preferred things to be tangible. He respected the possibility of a psychic threat too much to dismiss what the landlord said. Even so, he made one last attempt to remain scornful.

'Children believe in demons and devils. Peasants still protect something they call their souls. I am an educated man, and you're right, I have a job to do. What was this message? Tell me.'

'I've warned you,' the innkeeper replied. 'I've warned others, but they wouldn't listen either. Maybe those people at the manor have ways of steering a man's will towards themselves. Remember this: at present you have the freedom to get away. I've known of more than one person who has entered those gates, but I haven't seen any come back out. Unless, of course, they've done so like the boy, Cuthwin – half naked, the slave of one of their Superiors. If it happens to you, I will not be able to help you. Like I told you, I'm a landlord, not a hero – and I'm certainly no fool.'

'I hear what you say. Give me the message,' Denton said. Strangely, these warnings had the opposite of their intended effect. He had finally resolved to go to Tarne and damn the consequences.

'He wants you to go to the crossroads at the other end of the village. He says you'll find your Cuthwin there and he might need your help. If you take a word of that at face value, you're not safe to be let out of doors.'

The sun had come out, but it only seemed to illuminate the drabness of Tarne village. It was a weak, pathetic light and the small houses – once desirable, neat little places – now had the lethargic, unkempt air of the drunk who decides the day is not worth the effort of a wash or shave.

As he approached the crossroads, Denton heard the babble of conversation. He followed a bend in the road. Ahead of him was a small group of village youths. He had seen one or two of them in the tavern those past few evenings. Most were farm-hands or labourers and they were an uncouth lot. Their work had given them powerful bodies – most were tall – but they were also ungainly. They spoke in thick accents and had seemed to care about little, other than beer, work and women.

He was puzzled, therefore, to make out shouts of, 'Grab his cock.' 'Let's make him hard!' 'Have you ever seen an arse like that on a man? It's like a baby!'

He drew nearer. Morgan was with them. He pushed through the group and came to meet the newcomer.

'We're having a little entertainment here,' he said. 'I thought you, being a visitor to our village, should receive an invitation. Come with me and see.'

Denton said nothing. He had an inkling of what the 'enter-tainment' would prove to be.

He was not at ease with the village boys. They had laughed at his city manners before. They had even found his clothing amusing. He knew they were not anything to do with the community, so presumably they'd gathered without Morgan's say-so.

All this was surely a provocation of some kind and it was directed at Denton. He now knew Morgan was aware of his interest in Tarne, of his walks to the manor. He must keep his wits about him so as to guard against being led into the trap that he was sure awaited him.

'It's the fine gentleman from the big city!' one of the boys crowed. 'He's come to have a look at some boy-meat! Let him through, lads!'

They all roared with laughter and, as Denton approached, made mock bows and effeminate curtsies to him. This pantomime was so awkwardly enacted it could have been dismissed as childish, but Denton coloured and felt the insult deeply. Youths like this had always terrified him. He had never himself been through a similar stage of adolescent boorishness and he didn't know how to respond to it. When he was a teenager, he had been mocked for his girlish demeanour and had been bullied because he couldn't find it in himself to fight back when challenged. For all their faults, he had desperately wanted to be like other boys. This yearning found its expression in his solitary nightly gropings, during which he often recalled the beatings he had suffered at the hands of these good-looking bullies. He had used these memories to fuel his ardour, turning them into cravings which he thought he would never satisfy.

Now he was presented with seven such loutish youths. They were gathered around a pillory which, though Denton had not previously noticed it, must have stood there for years. It had a thick coating of moss; the huge, medieval-looking hinges and locks were rusted, though they were apparently still functional.

It was, as Denton had known all along, Cuthwin who had been the centre of their attention. The boy was shivering in the cold. He had been given no shirt to protect him and his trousers were in an untidy mess round his ankles. His skin was a mass of goose flesh and his eyes were screwed shut as though by not looking at his tormentors he might make his ordeal more bearable. His hands and neck were trapped in the ancient wood. He had been given a box to stand on, for the post that supported the crossbar had been intended for taller men, possibly even the fathers of those who now stood around it.

Cuthwin had been spattered with mud. In fact, one miscreant was in the act of throwing a cake of it at his face as Denton approached. It hit Cuthwin's mouth and he spluttered, trying to rid himself of it. The boy who had thrown it smeared the filth over Cuthwin's face and stood back to admire the effect.

Denton's appearance among them had quietened them a

119

little. They sniggered and whispered, but they were waiting for Morgan to take the lead. Maybe he had already told them they were to be treated to another man's abasement.

'This gentleman is known to the prisoner. You must excuse us, lads. I must apprise him of the situation,' Morgan announced.

The group pulled back from the pillory, first those closest to it and then the others. Their withdrawal was reluctant and they didn't go more than two or three feet away.

Cuthwin attempted to open his eyes. They were caked in dried mud, which blinded him for a second or two. As he caught sight of Denton, the relief on his face was pathetic. Denton knew he expected help to result from his presence there, but he was certain there was nothing he could do.

'What has he done?' he asked Morgan quietly. 'Why are you humiliating him like this?'

'Oh, he's done nothing – nothing at all. I just fancied our community was becoming a little bit insular. I know these morons prefer to take their pleasure with a woman's slit, but I wondered if they might like – how shall I put it? – "a sample of what they're missing" perhaps. I've invited them all to fuck him if they wish to. They haven't taken me up on the offer yet, but – you know what lads are – I expect they will. I intend to leave him here until he's been had by every one of them. It's the very least I can do, after all. He won't be available for much longer.'

'What do you mean?' Denton said. 'Why won't he?'

'How foolish of me. I didn't realise, you don't know. I thought perhaps you'd have found out by now. After all, you are a professional snooper, aren't you? That is what you're here in Tarne to do?'

'Like you said earlier, I'm a visitor. I thought we were . . .' The word seemed so inappropriate, but Denton chanced it: 'I thought we were friends.'

Morgan stood in front of him and held the lapels of Denton's coat. He pulled it from his shoulders, leaving him standing in his shirtsleeves. This immediately brought the villagers closer. There was going to be some more action and they wanted to be part of it.

'Barnard,' Morgan said to one of them. 'You're interested, aren't you? I saw the disappointment on your face when you saw how the cold had shrunk my slave's privates.' He put his hand directly on Denton's cock. 'This one's better, but we'd better check, don't you think?'

Barnard was encouraged by his friends' ribald cheers. He was twice the size of Denton. He had evidence of a slight beer gut, but this was nothing compared with the size of his upper body. His neck was short and thick and his jaw could have been chiselled from stone. He had sandy hair cut short in the way working-class youths thought was more manly.

He took Morgan's place and put his hands as Morgan had done. This time Denton's shirt was torn from him completely. This brought further whoops and derisive catcalling. Barnard raised his eyebrows and gestured with his head, inviting Denton to defend himself.

On his part, Denton had been transported back over the years and was now little more than the terrified schoolchild he had tried so long ago to forget. Though the horrid details of that part of his life were now safely lost to him, this scene had never been very far away from his consciousness. It wasn't something that had ever actually happened to him. Usually, the thugs he had encountered as a boy had laid into him straight-away. They had been satisfied when, incapable of withstanding any more of their kicks and thumps, he had passed out.

No, this scenario followed the pattern of his night-time mental re-enactments – a brawny hooligan was threatening to take him by force.

It would have been foolhardy to try to fight Barnard as the other was clearly expecting him to try. Denton decided to use the only weapon he had – his superior intellect. He could defuse the situation only by capitulating to it.

He brought his hands slowly round to his belt and undid the buckle. All the while, he kept his eyes firmly fixed on Barnard's, who scoffed briefly, but made no move to stop him. Then Denton undid his buttons and, still very slowly, still not taking his eyes off his oppressor, he pulled his trousers down to the ground. He stepped out of them and stood in his underwear.

Cuthwin shouted to Morgan from the pillory, 'Please, master! Leave him be. He has done you no harm. He's not one who you can use at Tarne. Let them fuck me as you said they were to.'

Morgan scowled at him and answered, 'Shut your mouth, you fool!' Then he addressed Barnard. 'Are you going to make this man show you up as the idiot you are? Take him!'

In order to stop Barnard considering this, Denton acted more quickly. He pulled down the white cotton that hid his sex from view, hoping the cold and his fear would not have the same effect on it as it had done on Cuthwin's.

Perhaps these lads had never before seen another man's organ primed for sex. Certainly they took an inordinate amount of interest in it. Like so many curious natives from beyond the far seas, they examined their prisoner's body as though it were a complete novelty which they could decide to kill or caress. One, more adventurous than the rest, reached to Denton's prick and touched it lightly with his finger. Even this slight action sent an anticipatory thrill tingling down Denton's spine.

Morgan spoke again: 'You have him naked. He has holes just the same as a woman has. Must I show you where they are?'

Barnard answered – he sounded less sure of himself now. 'We're not like you people, sir. It's not the way of us folk from poor families to fuck our own sex. That's something for the

122

rich who don't need new blood to grow up and look after them when they're old.'

He stopped abruptly. Denton wondered for a fleeting moment if this meant the boys were not going to show any further interest in either him or Cuthwin.

Barnard went on, this time confessing something he found shameful and doing so, not just for himself, but on behalf of the whole lot of them. 'It's true – we don't know what to do. Like I say, it's not the sort of thing we've ever been taught.

Morgan erupted with fury. He cursed in some foreign tongue which Denton couldn't place. Then he pushed forward, moving the villagers out of his way as if they were so many coats on a rack. He pulled at his own clothing, tearing the material in his haste. He looked ridiculous with his breeches fallen to his knees, his shirt tails flapping in the wind and his cock, which was monstrous as Denton remembered it, poking through the white cotton. Denton had seen men in the city looking like this when they took their pleasure with whores in the back alleys. These were gentlemen who would have been ashamed to be observed acting like dogs, fucking in the street, their apparel, the badge of their respectibility, messed – exposing their true nature.

'See,' he said, grabbing Denton's jaw and forcing it open, 'a hole – just like on a woman!' He turned Denton's back to them and pushed him so he had to bend. 'See – a hole. You should know that one at least – you all have one. It's not just useful for shitting out of.'

Barnard was not about to let go of his inhibitions. His friends, too, were wary of doing what they were being asked. Denton didn't care any more. He was going to get fucked, either by the whole lot of them or by Morgan alone. At least his ordeal meant Cuthwin was spared, for the moment, anyway.

Morgan turned him back round again and told him to kneel. He pushed his cock into Denton's mouth and fucked him hard into his throat. In other circumstances Denton might have relished it, but the presence of their uncouth audience made him ashamed. Behind this came an unmistakable thrill caused by the very shame that masked it. The act couldn't have given Morgan much pleasure: he was being too rough for that. It was an act purely intended to demonstrate his power. Denton considered what would happen if he brought his teeth down on Morgan's cock. He was tempted to, even knowing it would result in more suffering for himself. He resolved to be compliant and get it over with.

Morgan pulled out of Denton's mouth and prepared to enter his arse. The boys were curious when they saw him roll a sheath over his penis. Barnard said it was something he would never have done with his girl. Morgan was impatient with him.

'I could totally fill him with spunk and he wouldn't get pregnant, you fool. This is to stop his filth touching my cock. Watch what I do. You can have either of them to practise on when you're ready for it.'

He entered Denton's arse. Barnard watched, mesmerised. One of the lads from the back of the group pushed through, grinning at his companions.

'I'm for it! I'll have the young one.'

He undid his trousers and began pulling on his prick. It was not nearly as big as his bulky frame might have supposed one to think, but it rose quickly enough. Following Morgan's nod, he took a sheath and, with some difficulty, rolled it over his organ. Cuthwin steadied himself. The boy went behind him and, looking all the time towards his friends, plunged his meat into the available hole. Cuthwin closed his eyes.

The ice had been broken at last and the others soon lost their inhibitions and began to disrobe. Some were content to watch and masturbate, but four of them wanted this new experience.

With a satisfied grunt, Morgan came. He withdrew and

peeled off the sheath. He wiped its contents over Denton's back and smeared some over his face.

Denton was slowly losing his defiance and slipping into prurient abandon. He was made to lie on his back and pull his legs wide apart. His cock, heavy and stiff, lay flat to his belly. He grabbed it and tried to wank, but the boy who was about to screw him pulled his hand away and forced his arms above his head. He gripped Denton's wrists and lay on top of him. Then he hesitated, not knowing what to do next.

Denton found himself gasping, 'Yes, fuck me! Do it now! Take me up the arse!'

'He wants it!' the boy crowed. 'He wants me to use him like a woman! Do you like that big cock inside you, you dirty little she-man?'

He released Denton's arm just long enough to allow his victim to guide the waiting penis into the gaping ring of muscle, widened by Morgan and ready for more.

The boy soon found his position and began to thrust, panting and serious. His face was honest, plain and boyish, not yet marked by life's adversities. His clothes had the vague, stale smell of poverty mingled with clean sweat. Denton wanted to kiss him, but he would surely not have allowed it. He told himself he was to be this man's woman for the few minutes until the boy had emptied his balls. He couldn't do much but tighten his insides round the lad's meat and enjoy the feeling of being pinned under the weight of a male body.

The youth, on the verge of being a man, had pale skin with a profusion of adult hair covering his stomach, going down to where it bushed out at his pubes. This precocious growth slapped against Denton's own belly – his hips lifted to meet it. His desire to hold the boy and caress him, prevented by the iron grip on his wrists, kindled the flames of yearning inside his chest. He was lost to everything but the demands of his ardour. The boy came and another took his place . . .

* * *

The youths had gone. They would never admit to this event, not even to each other. When, in the future, the manor was talked of in their company, they would grow quiet or change the subject. Sometimes, when one would meet the eye of another who had been there, they would blush. As far as their culture dictated, each had sacrificed his masculinity for a few moments of animal gratification. What they had done that day was shameful to them. Nothing would ever be said.

Cuthwin and Denton, finally left alone with Morgan, at some point could have overpowered him and escaped, but they didn't. Cuthwin was too much the slave even to consider it and Denton still needed to follow where his demons led. He lay where he had been left, semen dried on his flesh where it had been smeared and dripped. He watched silently as Cuthwin was unlocked from the pillory and fell to his knees before his master. Then he spoke:

'You have me wrong,' he said to Morgan. 'I am willing to follow you and you must know by now that you may do as you please with my body. I will give myself to you and ask no more than you would give to this other slave.'

'You're not the right type,' Morgan said curtly. 'You can't enter our community as a slave.'

'Then what do you want from me?'

Denton was standing, reaching for his clothing, ready to put his sexual role aside and revert to being as before.

Morgan rushed at him. Denton didn't have time to prepare for the blow – he didn't even feel it. Within seconds he was unconscious.

Pascal

My attitude to Tarne was to change drastically. There is usually a catalyst that brings these things about and so it was in my case, but I will speak of that later. Since André's warning to me about Caspar and Morgan, I had looked for a way of provoking them in order that they might show their true colours. I knew this was foolish and André pleaded with me to be less stubborn in my attitude. I was obedient only with Leon. With the other Superiors, I became an increasing problem. Perhaps because of this, I was denied permission to take part in the group sex during which most of the other slaves were used by their masters. Leon had taken me to his bed on only three occasions since the first time. When he did, I had been forced to sleep on the slave cot at his feet, denied the strong arms around me I craved.

The rest of the time had been spent employed at my duties in the kitchen or caged below stairs with my fellow slaves. André had been something of a lover to me during those long nights. He never fucked me, but he allowed me to use his body in other ways and I let him use mine. We would take full advantage of the contact that was allowed us.

Mutual masturbation and oral pleasure had never seemed so intense and meaningful to me. André told me he thought this was because we were forbidden release during the day but had to spend most of our time in a state of awareness of sexual activity around us. We knew all the time that our main, perhaps our only, function was to be sexual fodder for our masters.

'The wanting makes it all the better when it eventually is given to us,' he said. 'If we spent our lives having who we wanted whenever the fancy took us, we would have tired of it and the whole thing would have become pedestrian and ordinary to us. The Superiors know this and they use it to keep us charged for when they need our bodies.'

Apart from this he rarely spoke of what we were there for or what the order was really about. Perhaps, after all, he didn't really know. I sometimes asked him questions and he would either ignore them or deflect my attention by plunging his large mouth on to my penis and making all other matters fade from my mind as I gave myself over to glorious sensation. After I'd come, he would ask me to do the same for him. By the time we relaxed in each other's arms, chained still to those who shared our pen, we would be past conversation and ready for sleep.

I detected that element of fear in his voice more than once. When I questioned him about it, he would simply repeat his advice to be obedient at all times and especially wary of Caspar and of Morgan.

An uncomfortable sense of foreboding nagged at my brain more and more. I tried to dismiss it as a fabricated atmosphere, created to maintain our sex drive. I couldn't ignore it though. André was apprehensive about something and I wanted to know what it was.

Caspar seemed to be feared by one and all. In the early days of knowing him and of first hearing about Tarne, I had supposed he was merely a procurer for the community. It soon became apparent he had a greater role in our lives there. He often visited, spending most of his time locked away in his rooms. When he was in the building, people whispered about it in awed tones as though he were some respected and fearsome dignitary who had descended upon us. I never mentioned our former friendship to anyone but André. I wondered if my friend was right and our whole time together had been intended simply to trap me into his web. He certainly never visited me or called for me to serve him or be beaten by him as I always hoped he would. Yet I still couldn't see him as evil. André had every right to his paranoia, but I didn't have to share it in order to love him.

Punishments were usually dealt out swiftly and effectively by whichever Superior was at hand. Nobody warranted any great amount of correction. All the slaves were obedient and at least pretended a desire to please.

Sometimes one would forget himself. Perhaps he didn't remember to say 'sir' or accidentally touched his erection when a master was in the room, before permission had been given. Then he would be made to drop his breeches to the floor. He would either be beaten while he gripped the back of a chair for support or, when it was decided he deserved more humiliation, the master would sit on the chair and make him bend over his knee like a naughty child.

We were belted or smacked with the flat of the Superior's hand, up to ten or twenty times. It wasn't so much the pain of being hit: it was the degradation of having to make our naked arses so readily available for it.

My obstinate attitude caused me to be punished more than the others. Each time, I felt my heart sink. With the slaves watching, I had to divest myself of my trousers quickly. Then I had to stand with my hands on my head while the Superior told me what I had done, why it was wrong and what he was going to do to me. My cock slowly grew huge while this admonition was given to me yet, all the while, my brain demanded I be a man and not give in to this treatment.

So part of me wanted to assert myself – I was as good as he was and he had no right to humiliate me in this way. The other part of me was demonstrable in my erect penis. As I knelt over the master's lap, I could feel the material of his breeches beneath my nakedness. As I bent further, my face close to his ankles, and the belting began to sting my arse, I knew I was not his equal at all. I was born to be dealt with in this way. I was a snivelling slave who deserved to have his arse whipped in front of the others around me. I wanted to sink further into that welcoming pit of self-depreciation, to admit my worthlessness by my total abasement. I would be made to count each blow or stroke of the belt until the allocation had been meted out to me. Then I would have to stand in a corner with my hands on my head, my reddened arse cheeks for all to see.

Such punishments could hardly be described as cruel or overzealous. Afterwards I was never sure which of the two of us involved had got the more stimulation from it: he for exercising his power to spank me, or I for being able to receive chastisement from whichever handsome boy had dealt with me.

These small gratifications were not enough. I had become little more than a kitchen drudge and I resented it beyond measure.

One day, I was drying and polishing the glassware which had been used by the Superiors at dinner. This itself was a punishment for my obduracy. It had become one of my daily tasks: the other slaves were required to do such menial jobs only once in a while.

I wanted more to my life of bondage than endless hours among the pots and pans. André, who was able to make love to me only with his mouth and hands, and Leon, who kept me at arm's length even when we were alone, were not enough for me.

My anger swept over me. The glass in my hand changed from being yet another object to wipe. Suddenly it represented the whole trick that had been played on me. I had given myself, expecting an endless orgy, and had ended up a skivvy. I was powerless to do anything to help my situation other than further demonstrate I was unwilling simply to accept it. I had decided to rebel: rebel I would. It was a simple enough thing to do: my hand simply opened and let the goblet fall to the floor. It crashed into dozens of tiny pieces. The entire room went deadly quiet.

'Pick up the glass,' said Cook, breaking the long silence.

'I can't,' I replied. 'I can't do this any more. I want to see a Superior, I want to see *someone* – now!'

'Oh, you'll be seeing someone right enough,' the cook said.

It seemed I was to be given no second chance to change my mind. I like to think I wouldn't have lost my nerve anyway, but it's possible. Cook nodded at another slave who ran off to find one of our masters. I stayed where I was, rooted to the spot. The cook came over and began to collect the glass into a cloth. He didn't throw it away, but put it on the table – no doubt it was to be used as evidence of my disobedience.

It was Leon who came to deal with the matter. I had hoped it would be one of the others. I knew I was going to find it difficult to keep to my resolve when presented with his reproachful look. Still, I told myself, he would get to hear about it soon enough, so best face him now.

The cook showed him the broken glass and added regretfully that I had refused to clear up the pieces and he suspected I had let the object fall deliberately. Leon listened and then beckoned for me to follow him.

We left the kitchen and I was led downstairs, through the rooms where our sleeping pens were and on to a small cell which was one of the several on a corridor beyond.

131

The door was heavy oak and the walls thick stone. There was one barred window, high up on the wall. It didn't allow much light to come through. In the centre of the otherwise bare room was a wooden chest and a cage, the latter just about big enough for one man to stand in with some small room to spare.

'Take off your trousers,' Leon ordered.

I pulled them down slowly, my eyes watching his face. He appeared to have no reaction at all. I was mortified inside – I kept thinking of a dog I once had which sometimes left piles of shit where we humans had to walk. When we punished it, rubbing its nose in the filth to remind it of our disapproval, it must have felt as I did then.

I wanted to say how sorry I was. I wanted to beg Leon's forgiveness. Above all I wanted him to say it was all right and he understood my frustrations and therefore forgave my actions, that I had been driven over the edge, that he would make sure I would never again have to resort to such tactics.

I was now naked, but not for sex as I wanted to be. I was naked to underline my shame. This time I would have to suffer more than a childish spanking. I was to be made an example of, I knew it.

'You will be whipped, and more,' Leon told me. 'For the time being you are to remain here to think about your misdemeanour.' His voice was not convincing at all. I could tell he was finding the whole situation awkward. He sighed and, in a different tone, went on, 'You must learn humility. They will not tolerate such behaviour from their slaves.'

It seemed odd he didn't include himself in this statement. He was, after all, as established in Tarne's hierarchy as it was possible to be. However, even André seemed to think of Leon as being different from the rest of them.

'Put yourself into the cage.'

I stepped inside it and gripped the bars. Leon shut the door and locked it.

'Hands behind your back. You don't deserve freedom of movement.'

I stepped backward towards the bars and put my hands behind me as he instructed. He took a pair of handcuffs from the chest. They were clumsy, old-fashioned things, heavy and cumbersome. He locked them on to my wrists, threading them through the bars so I couldn't move more than a step forward. Then he went back to the chest, producing something else from it which I could not see.

'I'm afraid I can't leave you any comfort. You must be seen to have been dealt with by me as you would have been by the other Superiors. Stay still while I plug you.'

I turned to find out what was about to be put up me. In Leon's hand was a huge wooden penis which had a large groove just before its base.

He didn't use any lubricant. It went in painfully, sticking on its journey up my bowel but relentlessly forced onward until the tight ring of muscle closed around the groove leaving only the base sticking out of my hole. I felt an urge to shit it out, but I knew I had to keep it inside me. I tried to relax my gut to make it easier. At the same time, I gripped the base of it with my arse to keep the thing in place.

'You will suffer if it comes out, so don't try to expel it. Of course you know that.'

He looked at me sadly and, leaving only a dim light burning over the door of the cell, he left me to my thoughts.

Five

D enton regained his senses slowly. He was in a dark place, lying on straw. He tried to raise himself to a sitting position, but his head swam and he felt nauseous. He had been clothed again, but only in his shirt and pants. He fell back on to the straw and rubbed his temples. He was vaguely aware of a restriction round his ankles. He shifted his legs and heard the clank of metal – they were chained together. The restraints chafed his skin, which was already sore from having been grazed in his unconscious slumber.

He forced himself to take stock of his surroundings. He had been imprisoned in a tiny dungeon. There was one window, which looked out on to the winding road that led to the village of Tarne. He must therefore be in the mansion itself. The glass he peered through was thick, with bars on the outside. The walls of his prison were thick stone and the door, heavy oak. There was a mattress of sorts in a corner, but Denton had been thrown on to a pile of straw, which hadn't cushioned his body against the cold floor.

His limbs ached and he felt better for standing, even though walking only a few steps was difficult for him with the encumbrances on his feet. At least his hands were still free and his body was only superficially damaged. There was a chamber pot and a tin bowl containing water. He tentatively sipped some of it and was grateful to find it drinkable. There seemed nothing else to do but wait.

He went over what had happened that morning. Cuthwin had been the unwilling means by which his captors had brought him here. The landlord had told Denton the message was a trap and, of course, he'd been right.

Denton still hoped the whole thing would prove to be some elaborate sexual game. He didn't regret what had happened with the village lads. He knew he would often bring it to mind when he needed some extreme scenario to imagine during the wanks he would have in the future.

Afterwards, he had freely offered his body for further so-called abuse. Why then had Morgan found it necessary to knock him out?

Strangely, he didn't feel frightened. He didn't even feel the need to try to work out how he might escape his present predicament. He tried to persuade himself he had at least succeeded in achieving the second stage of his mission. He had entered the mansion and at least would have more chance of finding out its secrets.

Though this excuse offered him a degree of self-respect, it was undermined by the pleasant anticipation of further mal-treatment. Since his arrival at Tarne, he had gradually realised he would no longer be able to skulk under a façade of dull respectability. It was too late to go back to the man he had been: he would always see his old ways as sham and hypocrisy. He might fool those around him into thinking him respectable, ordinary and totally heterosexual, but he would never again be able to fool himself.

They came for him after about an hour: Morgan and another man, Tristan. Morgan introduced him with sarcastic formality.

'Our guest has been kept waiting far too long. We must apologise. Allow me the pleasure of presenting my fellow Superior, Tristan. We have come to help you prepare.'

'What am I to be prepared for?' Denton asked, trying to be calm, but fully aware his nerves were taut and were causing him to tremble. His cock was awakening to the prospect of more abuse.

Tristan was slimmer than Morgan and had a more cultured appearance. He was young, probably not more than college age. Denton had had a crush on such a youth as this during his own years of study. He recalled his urges to go through the humbling experience of fagging for the boy. This Tristan might still use a cane to keep his underlings in order. Denton's penis hardened fully.

Morgan didn't answer Denton's question. He nodded at Tristan and said, 'We'll do it now. Are you ready?'

Tristan affirmed that he was and grabbed Denton from behind by his upper arms. He was strong, but Denton could have struggled if he had wanted to. Instead he went limp, letting his body sink back, supported by Tristan's. Morgan pulled Denton's shirt open to make the naked chest available to them. He tweaked each of Denton's nipples gently. Denton's chest throbbed briefly and pleasantly.

Morgan had a small box with him. He placed it on the floor and opened it. First, he took out a rag, which he doused in the water from which Denton had drunk. He wiped an area on Denton's biceps.

'We must be hygienic,' he said. 'This won't hurt you too much.'

He brought out a rubber tourniquet and fixed it round Denton's muscle. Denton squirmed for the first time. He guessed what was to follow, but it would have been useless to make any serious effort to escape it. He might have had a chance against one of them, but not both together.

Morgan produced a syringe from the box. He tested it and,

with an expert swiftness, found a vein and plunged the needle into Denton's arm.

Denton expected to be rendered unconscious again, but instead he was transported into a dreamlike state where he was aware of what was happening to him, but unable to prevent it or struggle. He felt no pain: he was floating, pleasantly tractable.

They laid him on the mattress and bent over his body. His mind was not caring of what they did. He was looking at their faces and admiring them. Tristan's proved to be the one that dominated Denton's attentions. His eyes were dark brown and he had very long, feminine lashes which curled upward. As the drug he had been given began to confuse his reason, Denton imagined this face change into another's. His phantom had returned to him.

The apparition leered through the bewildering haze and Denton heard himself asking, 'Who are you?'

He received no reply. Tristan returned to his sight. Though he was so physically close, Denton thought he seemed very far away at the same time. They were doing something to his nipples. Denton felt cold water and then pinching and rubbing. Morgan had hold of one and was rolling it between his finger and thumb, making it stand to attention.

Denton's cock was full. A hand, which was his own, but might just as well have belonged to another, began to grope it. Morgan didn't stop him.

A stabbing pain shot through Denton's chest. He realised he'd had his eyes shut for a minute or so. When he opened them, he saw blood on Morgan's hand and knew at once what they had done to him.

There was a tight feeling in his nipple. He didn't care. He lay back and continued to feel himself while they did the same to the other side of his chest. By the time they had finished, his hands were inside his trousers and he was masturbating. The pain in his teats was pronounced, but it accentuated his need

137

to orgasm. Tristan helped him by undoing his trousers and freeing his penis. Denton pumped himself hard, still swimming about in a fog of desire. The two boys left him.

He wasn't able to come. He couldn't hold his concentration for long enough and the rapid surge he was used to eluded him. Still it was comforting to feel the long, drawn-out warmth around his genitals and to allow the drug to do its work and remove all his cares. What had only just happened appeared to have receded into the distant past. They had pierced his nipples, he told himself. Even this seemed unimportant. He couldn't even raise the energy to feel the rings that decorated them. Sleep beckoned once more.

The slave merchant, Hazleck, walked awkwardly across the beach to where he could see the road. The cove was secluded, hidden by dunes. The fine, pale sand shifted beneath his tread and he cursed it for having the audacity to encumber his movement. He was fat and out of condition – any exertion was a trial to him. He was wearing unsuitably long robes which had already been damaged by sea water. Despite the cold wind, he sweated under the obvious wig he had planted over his bald pate. His stubby little hands, adorned with gold and vulgar gems, clutched his garments, holding them away from nature's irritating impediments.

His ship was ready to sail. It had not been a successful trip to the mainland. The slaves he had bought were poor specimens and he didn't expect to make much money from any of them.

This stupid liberalism would be the ruin of him. Whereas before he could have had his pick of dozens of beauties (not all of them willing ones of course, but that was not his concern), now he had to content himself with condemned prisoners and the odd fool who thought he might find true love as an Illyrian slave.

Hazleck disliked Caspar, with whom he'd dealt over a number of years, but at least Caspar seemed to know a decent body when he saw it and he realised its worth. Of course their business together was highly illegal. The men Caspar had sold to him had been acquired by dubious means and more than one had made futile attempts to escape, but that, too, was not Hazleck's concern.

A horse was fast approaching. Late, of course – Caspar's men never respected the value of punctuality. Hazleck shielded his eyes from the sun. Yes, it was them. The horse was ridden by Caspar's man, Morgan. Slumped across the back of his mount was the man he had brought to sell.

It would have to be Morgan, wouldn't it? He was far more avaricious than the others. Hazleck suspected he pocketed at least half the money that was handed over. He waved impatiently. Morgan acknowledged he'd seen his customer and spurred the horse on.

One of the crew came stumbling up the bank and asked, for the third time, when they might set sail.

'I told you, we have one more to load. He's here now. Be patient and think of the extra money you're earning.'

Hazleck liked to think of himself as a favourite employer of these rough sailing men. The truth, of which he was also aware, was that they ridiculed him. He had heard them imitating his plummy vowels and his lisp. He despised them, but he covered this, for mendacity was as natural to him as breathing.

Even in Illyria, the citizens avoided him when they could, but he still invited them to his home and acted as though each hated guest was one of his oldest friends. Only with his slaves did he allow his vindictiveness to show. They didn't matter: they were less than animals.

Morgan reined in his horse and dismounted. He didn't bother to return Hazleck's greeting. This insult did not go unheeded.

'He's not your usual type,' Morgan said. 'I think you'll find him more interesting than most.'

139

'You mean more expensive,' Hazleck corrected. 'Is his cock large? I like men with large cocks – they sell better.'

'Large enough. See for yourself.'

Morgan pulled the man off the horse as though he were a sack of grain. The prize fell into the sand and groaned. He half opened his eyes, showing bloodshot whites and widened pupils. Saliva dribbled from his mouth.

'He's drugged,' Hazleck said. 'How can I test him if he can't respond? My dear, I think you must drop the price if your goods are to be brought to me in this state.'

'You can test him well enough, you old miser.'

Morgan undid the man's shirt and trousers. The body was attractive and his cock was erect.

'Is that large enough for you?' Morgan said. 'If he can keep it up when he's in a stupor, he can respond just as well when he's awake.'

'Pierced I see. I like that.'

'You asked for it. Caspar especially asked me to do it. I think that's worth reflecting in our remuneration.'

'Three hundred discs and no more. He's past thirty.'

'Five hundred and no less. I know what you can sell a mature slave for.'

They haggled until Hazleck reluctantly agreed a price. The slave's clothes were taken from him: Morgan didn't want them, but he considered it a matter of principle not to allow Hazleck anything for nothing and Hazleck wasn't prepared to pay for them. Two of the sailors were summoned to carry the man – Denton, they'd called him – to the ship. Morgan left without another word.

'Take care, my dears. We don't want him to wake until he's been secured,' Hazleck fussed as they boarded. 'Put him with the half-caste in the lower deck, but have them both handcuffed to the ceiling supports. We don't want them to start fondling each other.'

★ ★ ★

Back at Tarne, Morgan was quizzed by Caspar.

'He's getting meaner,' Caspar said. 'Two hundred? Are you losing your touch?'

Morgan shrugged. 'Ten years ago he might have fetched a decent price, but men in their thirties are not half so popular as they should be.'

'Not so much it won't attract four times the amount when that foppish heap of lard sells him on. Are you sure you couldn't have done better?'

'Hazleck's a businessman,' Morgan said, defending himself. 'He refutes every argument. Anyway, you should be pleased. Denton is out of your way. I don't think we'll be seeing him again.'

It seemed like weeks had gone by. Throughout, Denton had been hearing the voices around him and, gradually, he felt his resistance returning. His body had been too weak to act on his impulses, but at least his mind was becoming his own once more.

The urgent appeals of his fellow prisoner brought him back into the land of the living. He stared blearily at the naked form across the cabin from him. It came into focus at last: a young man, perhaps in his late twenties. He was sitting, as was Denton, at the foot of a pole with his arms held fast behind it.

The half-caste boy had metal rings through his overlarge nipples and his throat was encased in an iron collar which had previously been attached to something – there was a ring welded to it. He had greasy black hair and, judging by the heavy stubble on his chin, he had not been shaved for some few days. His body was trim, a little on the thin side. His legs were long and slender and were chained together. He had fine, soft hair running down the centre of his torso and a long thin cock. He was uncircumcised and his cock and balls were rounded by more metal to keep him stiff.

'Wake up! You must wake up! Listen to me!'

141

Denton tried to speak, but his mouth was incredibly dry and he coughed instead.

'Do you know where you are?' the boy asked – a question to determine the extent of his companion's stupor.

'I'm being taken to the island,' Denton managed at last. 'I think they've sold me.'

'You know then. Yes. We are to be Illyrian slaves. Are you a convict or have they stolen you?'

'Not a convict,' was all Denton could say. He shook his head sadly.

'I stole money from my employer. They were going to hang me for it, but they said I had a choice. I deserve what is to come. You don't, and I am sorry for you.'

'Who owns us?' Denton croaked. He remembered seeing a hideous, gaudy figure and feared the worst.

'He's a merchant. Hazleck they said his name was. We won't be in his charge for long. Tomorrow or the next day we will be taken into the town with the others. He will sell us there. If you are sensible, you will try to keep yourself looking desirable. If you appear to be worthless or spent, you will be bought by some ruffian and used badly. The best advice I can give you is to act like a thoroughbred. Those who spend a great deal on human flesh will at least look after it when it belongs to them.'

Denton nodded. He looked down at his chest and for the first time saw the piercings. He thought he would find them abhorrent but the sight actually pleased him. His chest, so decorated, appeared sexual and he was proud of it. Yes, he decided, I am a worthwhile slave for some man to buy. I will give my master satisfaction.

No more did he worry about his masochistic needs. He accepted, then and there, that he was a slave and he determined to be a good and obedient one. Fate would carry him on his journey through life and he would not protest against it.

'So, I'm a slave,' he said. 'I don't care any more.'

His throat was still hurting, but he managed to shout out, anger and pain lost in the volume of his cry.

'I don't care!'

The shout brought somebody to the door. It opened and Hazleck's plump figure blocked the light. He smiled lasciviously.

'Well, well,' he rasped. 'Our little treasure has come to himself at last. I think it's time he did something to justify the inflated price I've had to pay for him.'

A thriving bustle of humanity came into vision as they were led up on deck. The sea was choppy; the rocking of the ship had given the prisoners the impression they were still at sea. In fact they were in dock.

In contrast to the dull grey of Tarne, Illyria's port was a blaze of vivid colour. There were sailors in their blues and golds; peasants wearing reds, greens, yellows; merchants in gaudy opulence; traders with bright waistcoats and hand-woven scarves. The seagulls barked overhead in the clear, winter sky. There was a smell of fish and salt in the air.

Here and there were groups of slaves, clothed in drab, torn rags and most of them in irons. They waited patiently. Those who were to be sold at the market would be priced and held in the stockyards. Those whose owners wanted a quick sale would be haggled over in the taverns along the seafront or nearer to the centre of the town.

Denton and his companion had been given some rough gowns to protect them from the cold. Their hands were free, but they still had to cope with the fetters on their legs. The half-caste, whose name was Sanjha, seemed to know the procedure very well. He whispered a commentary to Denton as they stood alone on the deck, waiting to know what Hazleck had in store for them.

'Whatever happens,' Denton said, 'we'll soon be out of his

clutches. I would rather belong to any of these people than to him.'

'Not me,' Sanjha replied. 'In my culture, we see beauty differently. Hazleck is not young and he may be selfish and spoilt, but I see underneath that. If I were a free man in my own country, he would be a lover to boast about.'

'You're not serious?' Denton almost laughed. 'You surely don't find him attractive?'

Sanjha nodded – his expression proved he was in earnest. At first Denton felt sorry for him, then he reconsidered. What right had he to judge another man's tastes?

'You don't find conventional attractiveness appealing?'

'I take what is given to me. If I were given the choice I would sleep next to an older man with some meat on his bones. If it is not to be, then my gods have told me I must accept reality and not wish for what is denied me.'

Hazleck came blundering on to the deck. He had been in discussion with some townspeople a little way along the harbour.

'It is arranged,' he said to one of the crew. 'Have them brought to the yard of the Adventurer tavern. I'll be waiting for you there.'

He addressed his two slaves: 'I've decided you two are to be sold separately from the other goods. You should be flattered, my dears. I am going to have to let the others go to market as one complete lot. I think you two will fetch a better price as a separate sale. If either of you disappoint me, I will make sure I sell you to some impecunious peasant who will make your lives miserable. So you see, we must work together in both our interests.'

Pascal

I had been caged for long enough. I knew this was the prelude to some greater punishment and I resented being made to spend hours chained to the bars, feeling my muscles slowly throbbing under the strain. These continual attempts to grind down my ego were creating in me a greater and greater sense of pride and self-worth. This was paradoxical in itself, but, moreover, my pride did not lead me to desire my release from slavery. It made me hunger for as much hurt as they could heap on me. I was able to take everything and anything, so why didn't they just get on with it and do their worst?

I started to shout out like a child in a tantrum.

'Come on, you bastards! Come and get me! Is this all you can think of to make be obedient? You can leave me here for days and I won't be any the more willing to wash your dishes for you. I want more than this! Give me your whips.'

My voice rang out hollow and unheeded. I gave up at last. I had been put in a part of the building where nobody was going to come within earshot. Maybe, I considered, they would leave me there to starve. This thought provoked fleeting panic, but I reasoned with myself. I hadn't done more than show a little will. Mine cannot have been a unique sin. Surely they must have come across such cases before.

Leon came back at last. His reluctance was still perceptible. He had with him some ointment. He came close to my cage and, reaching through the bars, smeared it over my back and buttocks. While he did this, he spoke to me. His eyes never ceased looking cautiously to the outer door of the cell.

First, in his normal voice, he said, 'This cream is to burn your skin. It will have little effect at present, but when you're cut with a lash it will make the stings the more agonising. Feel how I'm rubbing it into your flesh. Think about it, and about your stupid behaviour. You will be a slave. You will obey.'

Then he dropped his voice to a whisper and said, 'I don't know who you are or what you're doing here, but you've come from Caspar, that much I realise. Why are you behaving like this? Has he told you to do it?'

The warm balm felt good. It certainly didn't give any promise of agony as Leon claimed. I wondered if he had swapped the stuff he was supposed to put on my body for some other, milder cream. The words he had used made me suppose he was as fearful of Caspar as André. Could it be possible?

I had to gamble. He might just as easily be on Caspar's side. It appeared there were factions in every part of the community. On the other hand, he might, like me, have stumbled across the place in some accidental way and, though a Superior because of his physique, had a kinder, more gentle outlook than the others. His swagger, his rakish little beard, his earring – they might all have been deliberate decoys. Underneath, this man might be kind-hearted enough. I had every reason to trust him, but I also had every reason to suspect that trust.

'Caspar befriended me in order to get me here,' I said simply. 'I don't know why he wanted it so much. He hasn't spoken to me as a friend since the last time we were at his house together. I want to know what's going on – that's all.'

'Then you're a fool,' hissed Leon. 'You'd do better to keep your head down and wait. I can't save you from whatever they have planned this time, but in future, simply obey their commands and try to fade into the background.'

He checked the door again. I supposed the others must have been not far behind him. He gave one last, urgent piece of advice.

'You're not the one they want this year. I can be sure of that. Do as you're told and soon you will have cause to be thankful you didn't anger Caspar more than you already have.'

He had only just enough time to say this. Caspar entered the room carrying in his hand a heavy lash, such as the one which André had been made to use on me in Caspar's rooms.

He let it fall through the air to test its capability. Then he turned to me.

'This is not a game we're playing here. You will be sorry you have treated it as one.' He addressed Leon: 'Tie his organ tightly round. We will lead him by it to where he is to be flogged.'

Six

Whereas many of the other innkeepers simply allowed transactions to take place on their property, the owner of the Adventurer always provided something more. The drinking areas had low ceilings, the dark interior cut with shafts of winter sunlight which streamed through the leaded panes.

The yard Hazleck had spoken of was, in fact, a covered, flagged area in the centre of four groups of 'inner' rooms. As it was roofed in glass, it was unseasonably hot. Tables had been arranged around a central pit containing damp earth. This was raised some two feet off the ground and enclosed with barrier ropes linked to posts at its four corners. Twenty or so Illyrian men were happily gathered round the tables waiting for whatever entertainment was promised them. They were mostly regulars here, though it was only one of many public establishments that had been licensed for the sale of salves.

Hazleck had settled himself down with a glass of sickly-sweet liqueur. He had drawn straws with other slave-traders and had been pleased to have secured the first position in the selling order of the day. His customers would have more money to spend and would not yet have had chance to waste their wealth by purchasing somebody else's men. The other weaklings could be shackled together and sold cheaply at market. A quick sale to get rid of them. After all, Hazleck didn't want the inconvenience of having to feed them. He could afford to be blasé: even a reasonable price for these two would have made his trip to the mainland worthwhile.

The innkeeper's boy led the slaves in. It was traditional to keep the identity of their owner a secret but the satisfied smile on Hazleck's face betrayed his identity instantly. He didn't care. Even though he wasn't liked, his reputation as a trader was established.

The two men, now naked, were brought in side by side. Their nipple rings had been linked, all four together, by a long, thin chain. This meant they had to keep close together to avoid pain. They shuffled toward, dragging the shackles which weighed on their feet. They had been told to place their hands around the back of their necks and to keep their heads bowed.

The boy who was in charge of them had a paddle with which to guide them. Its sharp slaps kept them moving in a straight line towards the arena, though neither of them had dared to sneak a look at what was ahead.

He stopped them and freed the chain on their chests.

'Up!'

He had climbed into the arena and had unlinked the ropes. Denton glanced briefly at Sanjha, who was still keeping his head lowered to the ground. His floppy hair hid his soulful features, but his figure was beautiful. His brown skin seemed so smooth, defined as it was by the black hair that ran down his slender, sculptured chest. His sturdy legs and large feet were assuredly masculine against the aesthetic quality of the rest of his frame.

The boy leant down and slapped Denton's face.

'Don't gawp at him! Get up!'

With difficulty, they climbed into the ring. The earth was soft beneath their chained feet. It squelched slightly. The

149

potential buyers had already begun appraising them. The atmosphere had changed: business was about to commence. The boy placed the men in corners of the ring, opposite each other.

A buyer came close and, after gaining permission, pinched parts of Sanjha's flesh to test for excess fat. He turned to the table where his fellows were sitting and thumbed his approval. This brought laughter from his friends.

'As if you needed to feel it to tell. It's any excuse for a grope with you . . .'

The man took Sanjha's thin penis in the flat of his hand and tested its weight. This, too, pleased him, though it was soft, even with the band of metal still encircling it.

Several buckets of water were brought up to the ring, to the great amusement of those watching. Denton knew already what was to happen.

'You are to wrestle with each other. The gentlemen want to see your muscles and see them they shall.' The boy had learnt this speech: his words didn't sound at all spontaneous. 'Do not hold back, but any damage done to your opponent will be punished.' The formalities over, he reverted to his natural voice. 'Go on then, start!'

Sanjha lunged at Denton, catching him unawares. He was knocked over immediately. Sanjha fell full length on top of him and held his arms in a powerful grip. His biceps bulged wonderfully under the strain, giving his upper arms a powerful shape which was not evident when they were relaxed.

'We have to do this. They'll know if we pretend. Respond!' he whispered quickly.

Denton attempted to free himself but Sanjha was younger and stronger than he was and he found himself powerless. They writhed about for a few seconds. Groans of disapproval came from the audience.

'He's not what he seemed. He can't even move.'

'I hope Hazleck isn't expecting us to pay for that pathetic excuse for a man!'

Sanjha weakened his hold for a moment. He may have done it on purpose. Denton pushed hard and Sanjha was forced on to his back. The boy, close by them, picked up one of the buckets of water and poured it over the two naked bodies. The earth beneath them turned to mud almost at once. Denton gripped Sanjha's shoulders and forced him down into it. Sanjha responded by taking a handful of mud and slapping it into Denton's face. The crowd liked that. Some even applauded.

They rolled together, over and over, covering themselves with slippery mud. The boy sometimes kicked them gently to guide them into the wettest parts of the arena. When they found a dry place, he poured more lukewarm water over them, washing some of the filth away from their bodies and providing more of it for them to fall into.

Their chains made attempts to stand difficult but they managed it once or twice. Both now sported erections. They held each other, the slippery mess around their groins feeling warm and sensuous. Denton rubbed his chest against Sanjha's for a brief, stolen second. He wished he could be more gentle, make love to this boy instead of having to attack him. He brought his leg in between Sanjha's and tripped him. Sanjha fell with a splat and skidded about, trying to stand up again. Denton pounced and found himself sliding down Sanjha's body as the boy pushed on his shoulders. It was now impossible for either to maintain a hold on the other. Denton's face met the mud-covered prick and he took it instantly into his mouth.

The innkeeper's boy was about to stop this, but approving shouts from the audience made him desist. Sanjha relaxed, letting Denton suck him. His hands smoothed over Denton's back leaving a pattern of exposed skin beneath the mud.

The wet earth was difficult to swallow, but Denton managed to lick it off Sanjha's tool. He plunged his lips as far down as he could and used his tongue to stimulate the slender organ. It was the perfect size for his mouth and he was able to suck on it easily. Sanjha began to writhe about beneath him. He mouthed words in his own language: fast, desperate entreaties for more.

'That's enough.'

A kick just in time to prevent Sanjha's emission. Denton let the penis fall out of his mouth. Sanjha pulled himself upward from his waist and grappled with Denton's back and buttocks. He was now on top, and his legs were waving around Denton's shoulders, his chains dangerously close to the other man's face and neck.

During all this, the buyers had been using their own agreed method of placing bids. Some scratched their noses, others held up pieces of paper with figures written on them, most simply shouted the price they were willing to pay. At his table in the corner of the yard, the man whose job it was to keep account of all this suddenly rang a bell and pointed to the man who was now the lucky owner of Hazleck's merchandise.

The two slaves were separated and made to stand on clean flagstones while more water was poured over them to rid them of most of the filth.

The innkeeper's boy finished this task and addressed both of them.

'Your new master has other business to attend to. You are to be kept in the holding pens near the market until he's ready for you.'

He linked their nipples once more and they were hustled out of the place.

Caspar lay back in his bath and luxuriated in the warm water. Beside him was a table on which were a small handbell and a glass of wine. He took a sip, and was grieved to find a small piece of cork in his mouth. He rang the bell.

Troy came running at once. He had been in service at Caspar's house for some three weeks and had learnt it was not a good idea to keep his master waiting. He would have admitted, in the normal run of things, to the odd, deliberate indiscretion to provoke chastisement. He loved to be made to bend over Caspar's knee and feel the glow of a slipper against his exposed backside.

That morning, he had been promised that he would soon be taken to visit Tarne. From Caspar's description, it sounded a wonderful place. Troy had therefore been on his very best behaviour during the day so as not to risk being left behind.

'Cork!' Caspar grunted abruptly, holding out the glass.

'I'm sorry, sir. I didn't see it.'

Troy took the offending glass and had it knocked out of his hands immediately. Caspar pulled himself up out of the bath and grabbed his servant's neck. Applying gentle pressure, which was in no way resisted, he forced Troy down towards the water. He doused the boy's golden hair, then, briefly, his whole head before releasing him. Troy came up, spluttering and trying to rid his mouth of the soapy taste. His boyish face was contorted from holding his breath in. He forced himself to relax his frown: Caspar had told him he must retain that honest, youthful expression even when he was in pain. He began to pick up the pieces of broken glass.

'Leave that till later and get that shirt off your back. I've told you I like to see your chest.'

'It was cold downstairs, sir. I don't like to light the fire unless you're in the room . . .'

'I don't want your excuses,' Caspar said irritably. 'Ever since I allowed you to come and live here, you've whimpered and whined every time I try to correct you. Maybe I'm not demonstrative enough with my whip.'

Troy removed his shirt. His chest was lightly oiled so as to show off his pectoral muscles to their best advantage. His smooth body was perfectly shaped, the wide shoulders tapering down to his slender waist. Caspar pushed him round so he could gloat over the weals that crossed Troy's back. They were two days old now: he would have to find a reason to renew them.

'Take your trousers off too. I want you to wash me.'

Troy did as he had been told and, at Caspar's bidding, he stepped into the bath. It was easily big enough for the two of them. Troy took a flannel and soaped it. Lovingly, he wiped his master's beautiful, dark, hirsute body – the wet hair, flat to the skin, reminding him of reeds under rushing water, then the broad shoulders, the taut stomach and the wonderfully manly organ. He took special care over this, soaping it more than was necessary, trying to please Caspar enough for him to forget the piece of cork, the shirt, or anything else that might have displeased him.

Troy had accepted Caspar's ownership, but he hadn't wanted him to change into the bad-tempered person he had almost instantly become. He had imagined Caspar would treat him kindly, simply taking the dominant role in their sex life together. He, Troy, would in return take on all the domestic duties and consent to whatever light pain Caspar wished to inflict on his body.

It hadn't been like that at all. Sometimes it appeared that nothing would be right for Caspar. Troy wasn't clumsy and, God knows, he was willing to please, but nothing he did was ever good enough. Instead of the security he had wanted from being subservient, his confidence was being gradually eroded altogether. He felt clumsy and stupid. The sharp reprimands he constantly received hit home like so many knives. He was often on the verge of tears.

Slowly, he encouraged Caspar to kneel up in the water. He used his hands to wash his master's massive balls, letting the soap coat them well so they slipped between his fingers. He knew this felt good because he often did it to himself. Caspar closed his eyes and seemed to have temporarily mellowed his attitude.

'Good,' he said throatily. 'Good boy . . .'

Caspar fondled his penis, slapping it against Troy's hands. Troy, sure by now that these attentions were being enjoyed, leant down to kiss the head of Caspar's prick. It was warm and tasted of soap and bath oils. Troy let it run into his mouth and used his hand to rub at its base, still feeling round Caspar's scrotum while he sucked him.

'Filthy little pig,' Caspar murmured. It wasn't said nastily – it could have been a commendation. 'Use yor lips well. Your master's going to have to spank your cute little bottom afterwards.'

Troy's own cock jumped to attention. He accelerated the movement of his head to indicate his desire. Caspar opened his eyes.

'I've changed my mind. I won't do it later: I'll do it now.'

He pushed Troy away from him and climbed out of the bath. He stood impatiently, waiting for Troy to towel him dry: he did nothing for himself these days. When he was satisfied he pulled a robe around his shoulders and sat on a hard chair. Troy knew what he had to do. He wiped the towel over the front of his own body, not to give himself comfort, but to guard against wetting Caspar's robe. Then he collapsed gratefully over his master's knee, holding on to those strong legs and gently kissing Caspar's shins where they met his lips.

Caspar spanked him with the flat of his hand. The force of the blows must have stung him as much as they hurt his slave, but he didn't seem to care. Troy took each crack as though it were an expression of love. The pain across his buttocks burnt and stung but it had the effect of a gentle caress. His cock remained rigid; the pathetic urgency of his kisses, wasted on this inconsequential part of Caspar's leg, grew more and more desperate.

Caspar stopped in order to bring his hand underneath to feel Troy's cock.

'Just as I thought, you're hard, you shit!'

He rose without giving any warning, letting Troy fall off his

155

lap and on to the floor. The slave stayed where he was, on his back, the evidence of his sexual arousal obscenely on display.

'I know what you're about, boy. You like to be all cosy on my lap, even if it takes a spanking to justify it. Kissing my leg, rubbing yourself against my thighs. Well you're going to be disappointed.'

He made Troy stand in the centre of the room and bend over, holding his ankles. This painful stance made Troy's arse the most available part of his body. Caspar stroked over it – the flesh was still hot. He would give it even more pain. He would use a belt.

Troy's emotions turned to lead inside him. Right from the start, he had willingly let Caspar take the upper hand. His love had been genuine and he would have done anything Caspar had asked of him. Though worshipping the object of his desire from the lowly position of a slave was always going to be difficult, he had hoped he would at least be appreciated and sometimes cherished rather than scorned.

What was the point of carrying on like this? The attractive strong person Caspar had first appeared to be was all but gone and a belligerent sadist had taken his place.

The belt came down smartly across Troy's upper thighs, rapidly followed by slashes on his sore arse cheeks. He didn't try to stop the tears when they threatened and soon he was weeping quite openly.

Caspar didn't stop. He might not have noticed his victim's distress. If he did see it, he didn't care.

Troy fell forward, unable to withstand any more. His legs lost their rigidity and he crumpled on the floor, curling up and burying his face in the carpet, sobbing hard. Caspar bore down upon him and manhandled his body until he was lying face down, his arse still available to be belted. The punishment continued unabated for some minutes more.

'Is your cock still hard?' Caspar asked at last.

Troy shook his head miserably. He knew his hopes of going

156

to Tarne and being treated as Caspar's lover – even if just for a few days – were futile. Their life together was all for Caspar's benefit and he, Troy, would never receive the slightest consideration. It was time to be honest and to get out while the relationship was still in its relative infancy.

'I need to talk to you,' he said.

'Where's your manners?' Caspar rasped, threatening him with the belt once more.

'It's over, Caspar,' Troy said., 'I can't live my life like this. If you want a slave, then you must have one, but, though I'm submissive, I am a free man. I want love and care as well as hard sex games. You're not the man for me.'

There was a look on Caspar's face which lasted for no more than a split second, but Troy saw it: a look of unbridled fury. It was overtaken by a complete reversal of personality. Caspar took the boy in his arms and kissed him many times. He cupped Troy's face in his hands and his eyes were as honest as one could expect when he said, 'I'm sorry, I've been wrong. Forgive me.'

Troy wanted to. He wanted to believe this unlikely change in his master, but he couldn't fool himself any longer.

'I'm sorry, Caspar,' he said. 'I can't do it any more.'

Caspar rose and went to the door. He opened it and smiled.

'I'm sorry too, but I appreciate your telling me honestly. Go and get your clothes. I'll dress and walk with you across the fields.'

Troy bent down to pick up his shirt. He heard Caspar coming into the room but didn't bother to look round.

'I'll be ready in a minute . . .'

He was not given the chance to finish dressing. A foul-smelling rag was forced over his nostrils and, though he tried to put up a struggle, the drug took over his senses in little more than a minute.

* * *

Caspar stood over the boy's unconscious body, panting slightly.

'We couldn't let you go now,' he said. 'You've already been chosen. Animals who are selected to be slaughtered are not given the option of going home.'

Pascal

I had been suspended from a hook in the centre of a bare room. My arms, stretched above me, could just about take my body weight, but Caspar had put irons on my legs. Added to this, I had been lifted an inch or so from the floor. My naked body had been turned into a mass of aching pain. They had forced a sort of bridle into my mouth. It held my tongue back and made my jaw stiff. The straps of this were laced across my face. My head was thus caged in a lacework of leather straps.

Caspar had brought the cat-o'-nine-tails; the other two used switches of thin cane. Whereas the lash rained over my body, the thinner, harder cuts of the canes were concentrated in special areas.

My hopes of the cream being not the stuff it was purported to be had come to nothing. It had the exact effect Leon had said it would. It turned every abrasion into a burning intensity which lasted far beyond the normal effect the cruel swipes would have had.

They had clipped each of my nipples painfully and linked them with a heavy chain which pulled at me, making the clips bite further into my tender flesh. My cock and balls were tied round with thin leather and weighted. This again meant the forces of gravity aided my agony.

Such pain: it was more than I had ever been forced to take before. However, I had learnt to turn each ghastly ache, each fearful crack of the lash, into something more, something higher. I was, I knew, being tested and I was determined to prove worthy of it. I would not break down. I would never show tears.

This was what I had shouted for when Leon had left me in the cage. I had been sure I was able to withstand anything. I kept telling myself that, when they cut me down, they would treasure me as they had treasured no other man who belonged to them. I would be the one they would talk about as being better than the rest. I had more spirit, more staying power, I had –

The lash cut my back yet again and it was followed by a crack across my buttocks from one of the canes. I weakened momentarily. If I begged for release now, they would surely see I was contrite and give me time to recover. In the morning, my ordeal would be easier: I would simply be made to grovel at their feet, to say what low scum I was. Eventually, I would be forgiven.

Another crack. Its burning fire reminded me, I don't know why, of the falling of the glass in the kitchen. I remembered why I had laid myself open to this and gritted my teeth. I was no man's drudge. I was beautiful. I knew it.

The stings on my back, across my buttocks and the tops of my thighs continued. I was determined I wouldn't pass out for them.

The pain was now taking me out of myself and I was able to study the bodies of my tormentors.

Leon, even now as he beat me, was lovely to look at. He aimed his switch carefully and accurately, unlike Morgan, who was transported by his lust for causing pain. Then there was

Caspar – he didn't seem part of this. He was scourging me with every bit as much skill as I had remembered from before, but he was doing it without interest. I was nothing to him. It was this realisation that finally overcame my resolve. I began to weep uncontrollably.

'Why?' I sobbed. 'Why are you doing this to me? I was willing. I wanted to be good for you. I couldn't be a nothing in your lives. I couldn't.'

Caspar paused, suddenly aware of my presence, if it were possible for him to have totally forgotten it. He held his hand in the air to stay the actions of the other two.

'You are not nothing,' he said bitterly. 'You were brought here because I could not afford to leave you free. I expected you to be the one to bring Troy into our midst. You have already failed me.'

He aimed the lash at my back again and then let it fall to the ground without achieving its purpose. Suddenly he looked dejected. Suddenly I knew I was more powerful than he was. I didn't understand my power, but I realised, in that moment, there was a purpose to my being here. I remembered Troy and André. I looked again at Leon. They had all been part of some horrible scheme. I was part of it too.

My conscious mind gave way to the pain and I fainted.

Seven

André was fully aware of his ever-growing feeling for Pascal.
Their night-time fondlings were not the magnificent love
affair he had dreamt of when he was a lovesick teenager with
his sights set on a local farmboy, but they fulfilled him as much
as he could expect.

Unbeknown to him, things were about to change. Denton
had been captured and sold; Troy was already Caspar's prisoner;
and Pascal had taken the dangerous decision to find out more
about Tarne.

He knew nothing of what had happened to his friend and
had been surprised when he found himself shackled next to a
different slave that night.

On his other side, the man who was, as usual, chained to
him showed him no affection. This was hardly surprising: he
must have become used to Pascal and André being something
of a couple. They had been jealous of their love for each other
and had never let him join in as he had often wanted to.
However, the young, thin-faced beauty whom André found in
Pascal's place was tired and craved physical affection. He put
his slim arms round André's welcoming, manly frame and

curled himself into a ball in the middle of André's chest. There was little of him and André held on to his body like he might a small and delicate doll. Soon he was asleep, but his dreams were troubled with fears for his usual companion. Perhaps Leon had broken his habit and decided he needed an impromptu fuck. André hoped that was all it was.

The next day André was set to work early, painting a window frame. He would normally have enjoyed this: the careful attention it required suited his temperament. He rarely splashed paint on to the glass and could usually manage to do the job without warranting punishment for carelessness.

His thoughts were still with Pascal, however, and he found himself taking his brush over the line of the wood and on to the glass. This would mean a spanking that evening, maybe even the belt. Even as he considered this, he was mentally imagining Pascal being there when it happened. Pascal would give him strength to endure any punishment.

With a stab of conscience, André realised he was more in love with Pascal than he had thought possible. It wasn't just sex, though sex was important: it was Pascal himself. The wonderful, handsome, strong, caring Pascal, who had come into his life as a wretched slave, who had allowed himself to be lowered to a life of captivity.

Pascal had pride; he was not of a slavish mentality. It was strange, then, that, since the first time he had talked of escape, he had never expressed any further desire for freedom. André knew that Pascal was being used badly by the Superiors, but, though he detected a certain persecuted resolution in his friend, Pascal had not voiced it directly. Something wasn't right; something didn't add up.

Previously, André had always thought those of the community who had had no choice in their slavery were somehow more worthwhile than those who had wimpishly volunteered themselves. Now he was having to change his opinion. Pascal was not wimpish, but he had come into their midst of his own accord.

Of course, Pascal belonged to Leon and could never be André's lover in the true sense. For the moment at least they were chained together most nights and there had been no reason why this might change, though change it had.

André hoped he had not lost his lover for good but quailed at the thought of having to go to one of the Superiors and ask what had happened. He might even have to plead to be taken to where Pascal was. Having the temerity even to ask would warrant a severe punishment.

There had been other occasions when André had worried for his lover's safety. He knew there was something more to Tarne than this day-to-day domestic life with casual sexual activity thrown in. Every year at about this time, he sensed something big going on which few were party to. The attention focused on Caspar and Morgan. Last year, Leon had been with them. Once, André had heard screams coming from the west wing and had caught a glimpse of a shrouded body being carried down the back stairs. When questioned about it, he had sworn he had seen nothing and was a good enough liar to persuade his interrogators and escape – escape what? Punishment for accidentally seeing something? Or had he made himself dangerous to them because of what he had seen? Would it be his body they would carry down the back stairs next?

That day in the wood, when Pascal had been first brought to them, it seemed he was special to Caspar. André had supposed he was marked to be the one they used this time and the thought terrified him. There was little he could do about it. If only they could escape.

Two Superiors approached. They strode across the courtyard purposefully and came and stood very close to André. The slave continued painting, apprehensive, but not daring to do otherwise. There was a threat in the atmosphere but André could think of no reason why he sould be singled out – he hadn't done anything wrong, he was sure. Maybe it was the untidy paintwork, but he thought not.

Neither of the Superiors spoke for some time. Their silence was more aggressive than anything else might have been. It seemed to demand that André should know why they were there and should confess and get it over with. His nerves let him down and another streak of red paint smeared the glass of the window. One of the Superiors clicked his tongue slowly and shook his head. The silence continued.

André laid the paintbrush aside and turned to his masters but with his head bowed so as not to presume to look them in the eye.

'Is something to happen to me?' he asked. 'Did you want my arsehole or my cock? Or maybe you need to use me for your piss? I am ready.'

One of them grabbed André's cock through his trousers and pinched along it to see what state it was in.

'He's soft,' he concluded. 'Maybe he's been using himself a little too freely during the night.'

'You're to come with us,' the other one said. 'The Superiors of Tarne have some questions we want to put to you.'

They each took hold of one of his arms and almost dragged him across the courtyard towards the west wing.

The room they took him to was clearly designed as a torture chamber. Benches surrounded it where, presumably, an audience could watch the unfortunate victim being flayed with one of the many whips on display, or branded – though André was relieved to see the irons were not heating in the fire – or subjected to one of the dozens of other instruments of pain which were all about.

Morgan was standing in the centre of the room. He was stripped to the waist and seemed already impatient.

'At last,' he said as the party arrived. 'Did he try to resist?'

They reluctantly denied this had happened. André sensed they actually wanted him to transgress whatever rules they had conjured up for this unusual situation. Then they would have the excuse to punish him all the more and so satisfy their appetites. Being compliant and obeying every order in as meek a way as possible would frustrate and thereby annoy them, probably to a point where they didn't care whether he deserved punishment or not. They would torture him anyway. He couldn't win.

He was pushed flat on his belly in front of Morgan. Supposing it to be expected of him, he kissed each of Morgan's feet.

Morgan addressed the other two: 'I've been told to get what I can out of him in whichever way I choose. What do you think, gentlemen? Shall we have him suffer a lashing or do you think a slave with as broad a back as this needs something more entertaining to persuade him to talk?'

André trembled briefly. He would talk willingly if he knew what it was he was supposed to talk about. What if they mistakenly believed him to know something he didn't? He would have to suffer the extremities of Morgan's sadistic desire before they would possibly believe he really couldn't help them.

Morgan trailed a lash over André's back. It made him shiver and he could easily picture the damage it could do to his skin. He wondered whether he ought to say something. He hadn't been given permission to speak, but was he to be tortured without any chance of pleading his innocence?

'Please, Master, may I speak?' His throat was already tight with fear and his voice sounded hoarse.

'It wants to please ask us not to hurt it,' Morgan sneered. 'Should we let it say what it wants to before we begin?'

One of the two others suggested it might be a good idea to be fair to the poor slave. He ought, the man said, to be given the chance to avoid torture by complying with their demands.

The other seemed to be more on Morgan's wavelength. He interrupted his colleague in mid-sentence.

'No. I don't see why we should miss out on the fun. I'm looking forward to this. These slaves have it easy with their comfy lives – just the odd slap across the arse when they do wrong. I want to see a real man suffer real punishment. He's got the brawn to make it look good. Let's see how great his stamina is.'

Morgan ignored the one who was advocating mercy. 'He's a coward, very likely,' he answered the other. 'He will cry and bleat like a little lamb. These big ones are often soft. However, we shall see . . .'

'Master . . .' André began, but he was silenced with a vicious flick of the whip across his back. The two assistants lifted him to his feet and held him firm while Morgan stripped him naked.

'We'll rack him first of all,' he said. 'It will be most amusing to see that meat stretched a bit. Get him ready.'

They pulled him across the room and laid him down on the rack. It was ancient, but still in working order. André's hands were secured in the straps and his feet were anchored into two metal hoops at the lower corners of the table. His cock had grown hard despite his fear and he knew this would not help him. An erect penis would signify they weren't hurting him enough. He tried to make it soft again but he had to admit the situation in which he found himself was stimulating him. He didn't want the pain that would surely come, but he did relish the bonds, the chamber itself and the three dark, good-looking torturers.

He told himself to be as brave as possible and resist pleading for mercy or crying in pain. He wanted them to be impressed with him. Why this was he didn't know. He would be given no credit for it and would probably have to suffer all the more. They were clearly determined to break him. Pascal came to his mind and he knew he would want him to be strong. It was

167

more than a mere supposition: he felt Pascal's spirit there with him and he was helped by it.

Morgan turned the wheel and André's limbs were pulled a little. This was not painful – in fact it was almost pleasant: like stretching after sleep. He was left like that for a while.

One of the boys began to coat André's naked body with oil. Soon the slave's skin was slippery and shining. The tautness of his sinews was a beautiful thing to behold. The wheel was cranked up a notch and André began to feel the pain for which the instrument had been designed. He imagined all the other men who had been broken on this machine, all those naked bodies being pulled until the pressure became impossible and –

– and what? Did they die? Or were they released? Were they able to tell their torturers what was needed in order that they might be dragged back to their cells? Once back in the dungeons, were they left in chains to starve?

Another crank and the pain was becoming severe. Whatever had happened to all those other victims before him, André was sure of one thing: once restrained, there was little or no chance of their getting out without experiencing a lot of suffering first. Guilty or innocent, it didn't really matter. This was a thing built to make pain and he was going to have to grit his teeth and bear it.

Morgan took his hands off the wheel and stood back to admire his handiwork.

'What do you think, gentlemen?' he asked the others. 'Is he not a fine specimen?'

The nicer of the other two boys (as André was already beginning to think of him, for he had been the only one to advocate mercy of any kind) came round the other side of the rack and stroked the front of André's chest. He traced down to his navel and flicked the vulnerably erect penis with the finger and thumb of his other hand. André veered between extreme hurt and a kind of ecstasy. He was aroused, not just physically, but emotionally. He wished his cock didn't betray the fact.

The other boy stood by André's head and pushed his index finger into André's mouth. It was evident this was a sign of what he was planning to do later with his cock. He smiled cruelly.

'I think he's enjoying it too much,' he said. 'I think you should have flogged him first.'

'The thing is,' Morgan went on, addressing André, 'we've guessed what you and your little slave friend are up to. Oh, I know you weren't part of the original plan, but we've taken note of your closeness to the other spy and we're now just a bit curious as to what you're all plotting together.'

André knew they meant Pascal, but he had no idea what his lover had been accused of, or how he might best perusade these men of his own innocence. Further to this, he didn't want to say anything that would get Pascal into any more trouble.

'Nothing, I swear it,' he cried. 'Please, Master – Masters, I don't know what you mean. Pascal isn't a spy, I'm sure of it.'

'He knows who we're talking about then,' said the one by his head. 'That proves something is going on.'

'No, it's not true,' André protested and was rewarded by another pull on his already overstretched limbs. He groaned loudly but found the strength to continue.

'We were given permission to use each other's body when you Superiors had no need of them. I was chained next to him. He's the only one I've been intimate with. I'm sure he's as innocent as I am myself. Please, let me off this rack and I'll tell you anything I know.'

This last was a mistake. He knew it as soon as the words had fallen from his lips. The three of them pounced on the supposed admission with cries of 'See, I knew it!' and 'He does know something. He's admitted it.' Denials were now useless. He cursed his own stupidity.

SLAVES OF TARNE

Morgan spun the wheel the other way and his body relaxed into aching relief.

'This is just to remind you of how it is when the pressure stops,' Morgan said. 'You will be stretched again in a moment or two. That is, if you don't give us the information we need. Who is the man who was staying at the tavern in the village? He's in league with you, I'm sure of it, even if others here refuse to see it. You must know all about him, so you'd better tell us.'

'I know of no man, truly. I don't know anything . . .'

He was pulled again and this time the pain set in immediately for his muscles were sore. Morgan locked the rack and began to pace up and down by the side of it. The boy by André's head undid his breeches and took out his long and flaccid penis, which he pushed into André's mouth. He positioned himself on top of the prisoner's face. André was almost suffocated by the flesh, which now blocked his nostrils, and the cock, which stopped his breathing through the mouth. The boy eased off slightly, supporting his own weight on his feet so the prisoner could take in air through his nose.

The other boy was stroking André's testicles and adding more oil to the tip of his penis. Morgan stopped pacing for enough time to clip two large pegs on to André's nipples. He attached a chain between them and tugged at it gently. André tried to arch his back to take some of the pressure off but he could not. His arse was now the only sensitive part of his body that was not experiencing pain or pleasure, and he was torn between the two.

He decided to try another way of escaping their intent. He would spoil their pleasure by making them believe he wanted to be hurt more than they wanted him to be. As soon as the cock in his mouth was taken out for a moment he took his chance.

'More!' he hissed, through gritted teeth. 'Pull my body

170

more! I want to be racked! I need to be stretched and I need cock in my mouth. Please, Master! Hurt me.'

It seemed to work – at least temporarily. Morgan's face clouded over and he scowled.

'The bastard is enjoying it! He actually wants it!'

He cranked the wheel into its second position and André shouted in pain but quelled his scream enough to demand the machine be tightened further.

'Yes, sir. That's what I want. Give me more pain. I need to suffer.'

'Shut him up,' Morgan growled. 'Put your cock back in his mouth.'

The boy did so. André sucked on it the best he could, trying to give the organ as much sensuousness as he might, trying to make it seem as though he would rather be on this rack with this man's penis inside him than any other place on earth. He even tried to make contented guttural noises to support the illusion. Morgan exploded with anger.

'Get him off! I won't have the wretch gurgling as though he was in his lover's bed. I'm going to make him know the meaning of pain.'

They released the pull and then undid his arms and legs. He had to be lifted from the table because his body was protesting its discomfort too much to be able to support him. He was dragged limply to the wall and, at Morgan's instructions, he was chained with his arms above him, facing the stone.

The boy who had been attending to his penis stripped quickly and sheathed his own cock. He stood by the back of André and impaled him swiftly. André felt the penis slide into his gut and then the old familiar feeling of warmth as it plugged him and withdrew, pushing in and out. Each time the boy pulled out, André's whole body responded by anticipating his return into him. It made him feel complete, made him feel more than himself. Morgan soon stopped his pleasure.

'Either you're stupid or you're deliberately giving him what he wants, in order to defy me. Get your cock out of his arse. He's going to love that more than anything. We're not here to service him.'

The boy pulled out and muttered the only excuse he could come up with: that they usually did take slaves in this way and most men would hate to be fucked like a woman and against their will.

'He's not most men, you fool! He's a slave and he lives to be fucked by his betters. I'm going to make that pretty flesh sing.'

André heard the swish of a whip cutting through the air and, before he could prepare himself for it, he felt it come across his naked back with crack. It stung him hard and he clenched his jaw, hoping he would be able to stand whatever was dealt him without tears. It cut him again and again. He could only try to do what he had done before.

'Harder!' he shouted. 'Flog my back, my Master. Take my flesh and mark it with your lash. I need it!'

'Shut your filthy mouth!' Morgan yelled. He cracked the whip across André's skin three more excruciating times and then flung the thing down on the floor in disgust.

'He's not going to respond to this. But I do know something that will make him more amenable. In the meantime, you might as well fuck him if you want to.'

He left the room. André relaxed slightly. One of the other two followed Morgan. André was thankful to see he'd been left with the nicer Superior – the one who had fucked him. He came up close behind the prisoner and stroked his wounded back.

'You shouldn't have done that,' he muttered. 'I know you were being brave and trying your best to get out of being punished, but it would have been better if you'd simply told everything you know.'

'I know nothing, sir,' André wept. He was crying quite openly now, whether with relief or pain he wasn't quite sure.

At the back of his mind he was still worried about what was to happen to him. What was this thing Morgan thought would 'make him more amenable'?

'You really don't, do you?' the boy said. His voice showed surprise. Clearly, even he had supposed André to be lying. He had thought he could be persuaded to tell them something.

André twisted round to look at him. He was beautiful and his face had the kind of honest, open quality that made one trust him. He had very heavy eyebrows and these gave him a kind of eastern look, although his skin was not very dark. He had a small mouth and nose and the beginnings of a heavy beard over his square jaw. Like all the Superiors, he was hirsute and well built, but, despite this, there was something feminine about his appearance: gentle.

'I really do not know what all this is about, Master. If only you could tell them so. I am simply chained next to this man, Pascal. We have enjoyed each other's bodies during the time when it is allowed for us to do it. I don't think he is a spy but, if he is, he's told me nothing. I swear it.'

He felt wretched at once. This sounded so much like a betrayal. He had to persuade this boy of the innocence of both of them.

'They wouldn't believe me if I pleaded your case,' the boy said. 'You'll have to go through what they have planned for you and prove your ignorance that way. I'm sorry, but you are a slave. It is the way of things here. You have no rights.'

He had sheathed his cock again while he said this. His shirt was open and his trousers were down to his knees. He grabbed André round the waist and pressed his hard cock into the waiting anus. He rocked slowly in and out, dreamily muttering and biting the back of André's neck and nibbling at his ear-lobe.

'I like you especially; I always have. I don't usually have the choice of the best slaves. When I'm promoted, I will send for you to be my special piece of fuck-meat.'

'I do like you to fuck me, sir. It feels so good and I know that you're kind. Please use my arse as you want to. I'll try to make it tight for you.'

The boy became more urgent with his thrusts. He withdrew almost to the point where his penis came out of André's arse completely, only to push it back all the way with more force than he had before. André wanted it more and more. His troubles were forgotten for the moment as he revelled in the eight inches of maleness ramming into his arsehole.

He could tell the boy was close to orgasm and he wanted him to slow down so the fucking could last even longer, but it was not to be. The Superior spurted his load and sighed deeply as the thrusts slowly came to a halt. He pulled out.

André moaned as the cock was removed. 'If only I could fuck you,' he said.

'I should punish you for even thinking of it,' the boy replied. 'But I think I'll let it go unnoticed this once. You've had enough as far as I'm concerned and there's still more to come.'

The door was opened and Morgan stood on the threshold. He had with him the bruised and battered figure of Pascal, who crawled on a leash at his side. Pascal was completely naked and had evidently been whipped, judging by the stripes across his back and his arse. Morgan was wearing leather briefs, which strained over his bulging package. Other than these, and his knee-high boots, he too was unclothed.

He yanked his prisoner into the room and pushed him on to the floor. Then he grabbed André's chin and forced him to twist round once more so he could see the other slave.

André saw his lover collapsed with exhaustion and suffering greatly from pain that had been already inflicted upon him.

'Keep looking,' Morgan growled. Then he went over to the prostrate Pascal and began to shower him with piss. It covered him in an unrelenting yellow stream, hitting his body, his face, his hair, his arse – everywhere. Morgan seemed to have gallons of it inside him. Pascal writhed about under it, trying to keep the jet from entering his eyes. It was no use, of course, and he was soon a crumpled, wet mess on the floor, shaking and gibbering as the fluid subsided and finally died.

'He's not in a fit state for any more torture,' Morgan said. 'He's been under my particular care for too long. Like you, he's too stubborn for his own good. However, it might be interesting to see how much you intend to help him out when you have to watch him undergo more torture. Either one of you will of course be able to stop it simply by telling us what we need to know. If you persist with this ridiculous notion that you have nothing to say, well . . . who knows where we might end?'

Pascal

The last thing in the world I wanted was to have André suffer for my own recklessness. I had been beaten badly, but I had expected it to happen. They seemed to think I knew something, that my act of rebellion had been connected to some person they feared. I could do nothing to persuade them and I wouldn't have attempted to do so anyway. They might have betrayed something before they tired of trying to flog information out of me, and I still wanted to know more.

Now I had been taken to a dungeon and presented with the sight of André. He was hanging in chains against the wall and he had been tortured. I was prepared for anything else but this: they were going to use him to crack my resolve. I was manacled next to him. We were told we would be left to think about our 'folly' in not answering their questions. Morgan suggested this would be our last chance of reform. Then we were alone together.

Time passed: I wanted to speak, but was too ashamed of my actions having caused my friend such trouble. He didn't say much. At first he implored me to tell them what I knew. I assured him I could tell them absolutely nothing. He quickly

176

gave up and lapsed into silence. He was always like this: quietly reproving, but always passive. I wished he was more like me. Together we could do something: what that was, I had no idea.

Perverse though it may be, it felt good to hang there. My feet had been allowed to rest properly on the floor and, though my body protested at having been used so cruelly, I knew I had been as brave as anyone could have been. I had become more masculine: my wounds were a source of pride to me and this was the appropriate way of displaying my bruised nakedness. I shifted in my chains, the clank of the metal stimulating my cock. André was gazing at me, he too seeing the beauty of our bondage.

Eventually, a key turned in the cumbersome lock. I expected it to be Leon or Morgan but, to my great surprise, it was Caspar who entered the room.

'Well, well,' he said. 'Let's see if you're still keeping to your story. I think I might be persuaded to believe you, but I have to be sure.'

I muttered the words that were there in my head, but my mouth was too dry to be able to form them.

'Save your breath,' he said. 'Your fellow here has had to endure the rack because of you. Now it's your turn.'

He unfastened my wrists and I fell on to the floor. He made me crawl to the rack and place myself upon it. There was no escape and I knew I would not be spared by pleading, so I did as I was told.

My limbs were prepared swiftly – locked, not this time merely to restrain my movements, but so they would be the means by which my entire body would cry in anguish. André had not told me he had already suffered this. Now I knew it, I could only pray I would be as worthy as he had been. My torture would absolve me from being the unwitting cause of his own.

I lay there waiting. I wanted André to watch. I wanted him to enjoy seeing me racked. I resolved to make my tortured nakedness a beautiful thing for him to see. If I could endure this horror for him and him alone, I could do so willingly. They could do anything to my body – I had my heart, and it was safe in André's keeping.

And then there was Caspar. He might suspect me now; he might even resent ever having brought me here, but if I could show him how much pain I was willing to take, maybe he might relent and be my friend once more. André had to be wrong about him. I was later to recall this faith and consider how illogical it was. Even at the time, I was quite prepared to believe all manner of ill about Morgan. If one was guilty, surely the other must have been. I thought I knew Caspar. The truth was, I had known only the superificial image he had permitted me to see.

The rack groaned into life as he turned the wheel. I felt a pull on the extremities of my body and then a tightening about my chest as it was strained outward. My arms felt as though they had been yanked from my shoulder sockets and my legs as though they, too, were being torn from me.

'Effective, isn't it?' he said. 'That's not the half it can do. I'm not going to damage you, but I want you to know what we're capable of.'

'What is that?' I gasped. 'What is going on here? I know there's something.'

I was pulled further and I screamed as I have never screamed before. From where he was still chained at the wall, André shouted, 'Please, Master! Don't do this to him! He's not what you think.'

Caspar smiled, close to my face. He caressed my cheek gently.

'You have a true friend over there. Is he right? Are you not after all what we have supposed?'

'I am what I've always been,' I said. 'It is you who have not been honest. I thought I was to be brought here to be had by other men. I thought . . .' It seemed such a futile complaint to make. 'To have sex and to take pleasure from it. I am no spy. I want to be part of Tarne. At least I did.'

He laughed genuinely and I was comforted to notice that his attitude had changed. He let the winch take my body back to its normal state.

'I believe you,' he said. 'Yes, you're that naive. How could I have doubted it? You want to know more of Tarne. All right, so you shall. Tomorrow, at dawn, we will have our special celebrations. It is written: "The Three". Troy is one. It was he who brought you to us, not as I thought, the other way round. He brought the man, Denton, too. It follows. The prophecy was right after all. I should have trusted it.'

I couldn't make sense of his words, but my heart quickened as he spoke. It had been exactly twelve months since I had sought out Caspar. The Night of Orion was upon us.

We were taken into a great hall where a table had been laid for a feast. Pillars supported the ceiling at regular intervals. We were each bound to one of these, our hands behind, ropes across our chests and upper legs and our feet hobbled: iron bars linking them together. We might have been placed there as observers or as human decorations. The flickering light turned André's beauty into a statuesque simplicity. He was all dark shadows, highlighted in red and gold. I knew the burning torches illuminated my restrained body in the same way. Caspar left us.

The Superiors arrived in groups of twos and threes, about twenty people altogether. I recognised some, but there were many I had never set eyes on. They took their places at the table. Not one of them paid us the slightest attention. Candles were lit and an air of festivity was all about. The Superiors laughed and joked together, quietening as one of their number banged the table to draw their attention to the entrance of Caspar, Leon, Morgan and another slave.

This last person was dressed in a robe made of coarse, white fabric and had a sack over his head. His hands were tied in front of him and he stood silently where he was told: on a dais at the top end of the room. Caspar felt his crutch through the material to check his penis and seemed satisfied with what he found. Then he addressed the assembly.

'There has been danger in our midst, but it is past. By dawn tomorrow, the crucial time will have come and gone. Those who might have threatened us are unable to do so. The Lord of Tarne has looked after his own. Let us drink to him.'

They raised their glasses and muttered the toast he gave them. I could tell only very few of their number actually believed Caspar's grandiose notions of this 'Lord of Tarne'. It occurred to me that most of them humoured him in order to enjoy their own sex in the way they wanted. This was no 'order' or 'community': it was an autocracy, controlled by fear of the unknown.

'As always,' Caspar continued, 'I have been led towards my Lord's choice of boy. He is to be greatly honoured, for he will, tonight, give himself completely. So, our lives together will be blessed.'

He pulled the sack off the prisoner's head. There, pale and frightened, this 'Lord's choice of boy' stood before them. It was Troy.

They eased the gown off him slowly, exposing his flesh bit by bit. First, his shoulders and chest became visible. Then he was almost half naked, his bound hands preventing the shift from falling further. I remembered Caspar telling me how he liked nudity to be a hidden thing: clothes could tantalise the observer's appetites. He was right: Troy was so much more beautiful in his half-stripped state. He was exposed, whereas we were simply naked. He shivered slightly.

He was brought to the head of the table and made to bend over it. Caspar put his hand under the robe at the back and felt between his legs again. Troy moved uncomfortably, but didn't try to stop it.

'The boy's hard,' Caspar announced.

The other Superiors were hushed and serious. They watched intently, not moving or taking their eyes from Troy.

Briefly he was made to stand while his hands were untied. In the doing of this, the gown fell to the floor. It was removed, leaving him naked at last.

Morgan and Leon each took one of his arms and pushed him down over the table once more. I had been able to glimpse his nude body for only a moment or two, but it was everything I had imagined it to be. He was much broader than his clothed appearance suggested. He had, in fact, the body of an athlete with the face of a young boy. His skin was smooth and I guessed it was tanned, though the torchlight probably made it look more so than it actually was. He still had the long, thick, fair hair that he'd had at the party. As he spread his strong arms outward, I noticed that he had a tuft of golden hair under each one. His pubes, too, were still there: they hadn't shaved him.

I looked across at André. He was an older version of this same vision. Where Troy was supple and graceful, André was strong and powerful. His beard added to the look of maturity, as did the hair, such as it was, on his chest. He was still amazed by what was happening to him. He hadn't asked for any of this or deserved it as I had. For my part, I was intrigued and worried at the same time. Troy had no doubt been persuaded into all this in the same way as I had myself. He was already, perhaps, getting more than he had bargained for, and who was to tell what lay in store for him?

Morgan greased the prisoner's arse. He didn't care that he hurt him by doing it. I could see the cruel smile of satisfaction on his face as he pushed his finger deep into the boy and watched him wriggle as it invaded him.

181

Then, one by one, the Superiors of Tarne stood and removed their clothing. The three at the top of the room were first, but it wasn't long before every man there was naked. It was a sight to behold: so many men, all slightly different in their own ways, but each with the same physical attributes. They could have been all of one family. It was starting to make sense. This was Caspar's self-created family: he had surrounded himself with 'brothers' who would be in fear and awe of him so he could always feel safe.

I had never seen the Superiors touch each other before that night. Now they were doing so. They were kissing and embracing, stroking each other and fondling whoever presented their genitals near to hand.

Caspar was the first to enter Troy. He took him roughly, his thrusts causing the boy to be pushed uncomfortably against the table. Troy kept his arms spread and didn't complain. Then it was Leon's turn. He was slower and more gentle. I still couldn't see his role in all this. He was a respected and feared Superior who, in his turn, appeared to be wary of Caspar and to suspect him as much as André did. He was a dominant person, but he wasn't ruthless. How had he achieved his position of authority? Morgan, who was waiting his turn, had an expression of undisguised hatred on his face. I thought at first this was directed at Troy, but I soon realised where his focus rested and it puzzled me more and more.

Leon patted Troy's head as he withdrew finally. He didn't appear to have taken any pleasure from having fucked him. He had done it because he had to. I thought I saw him say something under his breath – a word of comfort perhaps?

I'd supposed Troy's ordeal would stop with Morgan. He ground his hips against the boy's arse like an animal on heat. He had one hand on the back of Troy's head and used it to support his own weight. Troy was forced against the table painfully. His arse must have been losing its resistance now and I hoped Morgan's brutal stabbing would not be as uncomfortable for him as it might have been. He came at last and pulled out, his softening penis still oozing come into the sheath. He pulled it off and cast it aside. I tensed. Would they take Troy away now?

It was not to be. Troy's poor arse was fucked by every one of them. Some of the younger ones were gentle with him and some I wouldn't have objected to having inside me. Most were happy to follow Morgan's and Caspar's examples and use Troy as a fuck-hole, taking no account of his hurt. His ordeal lasted for over an hour. By the end of it, he was barely able to move; there was no necessity to bind his hands again, but bind them they did. He was clothed again, blindfolded and taken from the room. Caspar and Morgan went with him.

Leon sat alone at the end of the table and picked at a bowl of fruit. The others tucked into their meal with gusto. One or two near us took some delight in throwing bones, apple cores and half-eaten vegetables at us. They didn't speak to us directly: our genitals were the most obvious and favourite targets. I hated it. I could have coped with being on display as a handsome prisoner, valued for my looks, but this denigrated me, leaving me shameful and filthy. Worse, I had to see André, who deserved to be caressed and cherished, hanging his head miserably. My heart went out to him. A boy left his chair and, correcting André's position, took a few steps back and let him have a handful of mess full in his face.

It wasn't to be for long. When they had finished eating, all but Leon left. I had thought we would be screwed as Troy had been. I wanted it, for watching his ordeal had made me burn with pent-up sex. I needed to come. I would have begged for it.

Leon looked around swiftly in that same stealthy way he had when I was locked in the cage and he had asked me about my relationship with Caspar. He was not one of them, I was sure of it now. He walked swiftly across the room towards us.

'Do you trust me?' he asked quickly.

We were being addressed as human beings once more and it was difficult to respond as immediately as his tone suggested we should.

'Quickly,' he said. 'Yes or no. We have little time.'

I said that I did. André nodded as soon as I had spoken. As always, he was too subservient to do anything other than follow.

'Tonight is the Night of Orion. If I don't strike now, all will be lost. I can't explain, but it's crucial you come to the altar. I'll give you directions. Will you do as I ask?'

While he was saying this, he was untying us. I agreed to his demands. Then we heard footsteps.

'Quick,' said Leon. 'Whoever it is mustn't suspect. Get on your knees and suck my cock.'

He had it out of his breeches in an instant and I took it hungrily into my mouth. My own hard-on was raging between my legs. I contented myself with the warmth of Leon in my throat. André was standing, helpless, not knowing what was required of him.

'Lick his arse, you fool – anything,' Leon hissed.

André dropped to his knees and buried his face in my buttocks. Soon I felt the gentle rasping of his tongue as it found my hole and probed into it. I pushed towards him and was rewarded with the slippery sensation as he licked inside me. I closed my eyes.

It was one of the Superiors, but a youngster and not one we had reason to fear. Leon outranked him and he would never have dared question his decison to use the two of us in whatever way he wanted.

'When you've had your pleasure, sir, Caspar wishes you to go to him. He says it's important.'

Leon nodded and the boy vanished.

'He won't think what he's seen is important enough to gossip about,' Leon said.

He took his cock from my mouth. André stopped his probing of my arse and I was bereft.

'You must follow my instructions exactly,' said Leon, looking at me. 'For some reason, Caspar fears you. Maybe you're there in his book of fortune . . .' He held up his hand to prevent my questioning his words. 'It doesn't matter. Suffice it to say, I truly believe you're one of a few people who must stop this place from descending into hell.'

He kissed me with an intensity that displayed more than love. He was letting me know that what we were about to embark upon would be a fight to the death.

Eight

Hazleck finished his business with his customer. Denton couldn't hear the details of it, but he saw a weighty bag of coins exchange hands. The man who had bought them was polite, but curt. He was evidently rich and chose, like Hazleck, to wear obvious and tasteless signs of his wealth: he practically clanked with gold jewellery. He was in his late fifties, sharp-boned and tight-lipped. He had a mass of grey hair and wore rouge and eye shadow. His nails were manicured and, even at a distance, the smell of sickly perfume reached Denton's nostrils. Hazleck came bustling over, pleased with himself and bursting with satisfaction – his slaves had been worth waiting for.

'Now, my children,' he oozed, 'though to be accurate, you're not *my* children any more, are you? This is mine instead!' He jangled the bag of coins. 'You'll be pleased to know you'll be seeing me again. You're to be taken to a brothel and used as whores. I hope you like the prospect and will give your new owner satisfaction. He will want a chance to gain back some of his money and I must allow it him. I fully intend to visit you from time to time.'

Sanjha's cock hardened; Hazleck crowed.

'Good! You will make a fine whore for our friend.' He put his fat face close to Denton's and rasped, 'You'd be well advised to follow this slave's example and get your penis into the right shape for the task ahead. There are ways of making you agreeable, but I don't think you'd like them very much.'

'You're a fool,' Denton said. Hazleck's expression clouded over and he gripped Denton's cheeks between his fingers, squeezing them painfully.

'I'm a what?'

'You could have so much, but you prefer to take money instead. Don't you realise that you've just sold your chance of having a man to love you?'

Denton wasn't sure of what he was saying – the words came into his head unbidden. He was aware only of Hazleck's immediate change of attitude and Sanjha's unspoken wish that he continue.

'What do you mean, my impudent pretty one?'

'I must speak with you properly. It isn't on my account, believe me. Will our new owner allow us ten minutes?'

Hazleck looked across to the table where the man was frowning suspiciously. He waved across to indicate all was well, but the man was having none of it.

'They're mine, stop pawing them,' he said.

Hazleck simpered. 'Would you permit me to say goodbye to this one? I will only take a few moments and then I'll bring him over to your brothel myself.'

The man refused. If Hazleck wanted to have further discourse, he would have to pay the going rate and visit Denton in his new place of work.

'His time belongs to me and it must be paid for,' he said. 'You would insist on as much if I had sold him to you.'

'Are you saying you don't trust me, my friend? I will bring him and directly.'

'He's coming with me now,' said the other. 'If you want to kiss him goodbye it will cost you.'

He put a halter round each slave's neck and dragged them away. Hazleck called after them.

'Very well, I'll finish what business I have and come to the whorehouse. Have him ready for me and I'll pay you.'

On the way, Denton formulated what he would say when he was able to speak to Hazleck. It might mean he would be forced to screw the man, or worse, be screwed by him. Whatever happened there was little chance it would do him any good, but it might at least help Sanjha.

The brothel was below ground. Its rooms glowed with pink and blue lights. Cushions were scattered about the floor and small alcoves were curtained off where the customers could take their choice of boy for half an hour at a time. The two new whores were brought in and their owner instructed two painted youths to 'make them ready'.

Denton was taken to a pool of frothing warm water and told to get in. The boy who had been allocated to him was in his late teens and would have been beautiful if his natural features had been allowed to show through the make-up on his face. As it was, he appeared cheap and crude. He was in keeping with his surroundings, but it was a shame to spoil his looks. Underneath the paint his black eyes shone with a lustre that needed no embellishment. His eyelids were heavy and rounded, giving him a wise appearance, like some Indian god. This grace was also present in his general physique, which would not have disgraced a temple statue. He moved with a leonine elegance, careful and smooth in his every step. He had a heavy foreign accent which appealed to Denton instantly.

'I am Ghani,' he said, casting off a muslin gown which had covered him. 'You will permit me?'

He climbed into the water and washed all the remaining

mud from Denton's body. It was soothing to feel his hands. Denton abandoned himself to the seductive ministrations. Ghani was careful; he took his time, making his task sensuous and loving.

'Your body is nice,' he said. 'You will have many customers wanting to fuck you.'

Denton didn't reply. He was tired and wanted to enjoy these few moments of relaxation. He fingered the boy's cock idly. It was circumcised, thin and long. Ghani smiled.

'I have nice penis? You like it? We are not permitted to use each other until a customer wants to watch us do it, but that happens very often. I will fuck you soon, yes?'

Denton took his hand away and nodded. 'Soon, yes,' he said.

'Now you must be painted like me,' Ghani went on. 'Dry yourself and lie on the rug. I will make you look more beautiful.'

Denton had guessed this was to happen. He did as he had been asked. Ghani knelt beside him and, with much concentration, applied rouge, mascara, lipstick and eyeliner. He took all the care of an artist and it was a good fifteen minutes before he was satisfied. He reddened Denton's nipples too, and playfully applied more rouge to his cock.

'We must be like the peacock,' he explained. 'Colours are sexual, do you not agree?'

Denton thought it churlish to contradict him. He liked Ghani. He wanted him to be pleased with his work, the distasteful results of which were, after all, only temporary.

'If I must be a whore, I must look like one,' he said.

Ghani held up a mirror. Denton was truly surprised. He had been transformed into an exotic creature with arched brows and deep eyes. His lips were red – but a dark, royal red, which was shaped expertly to give them their full effect. Even his eyelashes were luscious and mysterious. He smiled.

'It isn't me,' he said softly. 'You have made me beautiful.'

'You were beautiful before,' Ghani replied. 'I can improve on nature, but I can't alter it beyond recognition. I hope you like what I have done.'

Denton kissed him. He looked shocked for a moment and then responded fully. He leant back and grinned charmingly.

'Soon I will fuck you, but we must wait. I fear you must be taken away from me now. Try to please and you will not suffer.'

Denton took the boy's hand and allowed himself to be taken back to the main room. He was ushered, with many strokes and much patting, into one of the booths. There was an oversoft bed – big enough for two, but only just – and a cabinet, which presumably contained the things a customer would need in order to fuck him. He didn't bother to look. He lay back on the bed and closed his eyes. At least his body would be looked after here: it would not make sound business sense to mark him in any way.

His new owner came to look at him, but he said nothing. He didn't require Denton to do anything more than turn over to allow one of the man's fingers into his anus. He was prodded for a short time, not unpleasantly. His own hand was placed against his penis. He gathered he was to make himself hard again. He tried to, but found he was too tired.

The brothel keeper sat on the edge of the bed and pulled gently at Denton's nipple rings. This had some effect, but he still couldn't manage a full erection. The man ran his finger over the sensitive head of Denton's cock and continued to tweak his nipples. Denton closed his eyes and tried to imagine another person doing this to him. He was going to have to live in his imagination a lot if he was going to survive this. He drifted for a moment or two, allowing the feeling to build in his chest and at his cock. Faces moved in and out of his mind: Ghani, Sanjha, Morgan, Cuthwin . . . Then, all at once, his ghost returned to him, grinning cruelly and full of hate.

'You're life is spent,' it said. 'You are nothing and will never know freedom again. Your body has been taken from you and will be sold to men so they can rid themselves of their spunk.'

He opened his eyes to dismiss the vision. Hazleck was there, standing behind Denton's owner. It was the owner who had spoken through Denton's dream.

'This man has paid me back to have you. You will do as you are told and please him.'

Hazleck had taken off his outdoor clothing and covered himself in a muslin gown such as the one Ghani had worn.

'If he can't get hard, I'll need a reduction in your rates,' he said.

The brothel keeper had obviously given up trying to stimulate him. 'If he can't get a hard, it's because you used him before he was sold to me. Either that, or you've allowed him to wank himself. Try again, fat man.'

'Really, there's no need for such insults. I am stringent in making sure my goods don't have an opportunity to use themselves and I certainly have not had him myself. No matter. Leave us alone. I'm paying for this time.'

The man left. Hazleck sat down on the edge of the bed.

'I'm not a bad man,' he said. 'I will make very few demands upon you.'

'You haven't come to use my body,' Denton whispered. 'You want to know what I meant earlier.'

Hazleck tutted. 'You must rid yourself of that wilful nature. It doesn't do for a whore-slave to contradict. You're impertinent.'

He planted his lips around Denton's half-soft cock and sucked expertly. Denton closed his eyes and lay back. He would have to get used to this being done to him by all sorts of men. Their attractiveness could no longer be an issue.

Hazleck's sucking brought Denton's penis back to its full length. As soon as he felt it harden in his mouth, Hazleck let it go. He smiled.

191

'I have lost none of my expertise. Sometimes you will find those of us who are not so conventionally good-looking have skills the young ones have not yet mastered. I guarantee I could play your whole body like an instrument. You would respond to my music, even though your eyes tell you I'm ugly.'

'It's not me you should be spending your time with. It's the half-caste, Sanjha,' Denton said suddenly.

Hazleck raised his eyebrows.

'He told me,' Denton said. 'It's not for you I'm repeating his words, nor for myself. It's for him. He's no whore. He is kind and gentle and he doesn't see you as ugly. He might even be able to have an effect on your manner, though I doubt it.'

This last comment resulted in a hard slap across Denton's face. Hazleck had heard him though and he was considering the idea.

'I would like a boy to love me. Yes it would be good. You are sure he finds my body attractive? There are many who would think him mad for it.'

'You're under no illusions,' Denton said. 'You're not for most men, but here there is a chance. Somebody who you would treat well. Somebody who would always be there for you. He sees you differently, even from the way you see yourself. I urge you to take advantage of it.'

'It will cost me,' Hazleck said. 'I will have to pay twice as much to have him back.'

'What good is money unless your life can be lived to the full? You're not happy, I can tell. Buy him back and give yourself a chance of redemption.'

Hazleck patted Denton's hand. Underneath the make-up, he looked sad and alone. Denton actually felt sorry for him. He was just another lonely man, trying to find comfort. If only he could be given the imagination to see the harm he did to others, he might have a chance of a decent life.

'I am grateful to you,' Hazleck said. 'You have nothing to

gain by what you have just done. Unless you expect me to spend the rest of my profits and give you your freedom.'

This had, of course, occurred to Denton as a possibility, but to say so would bring back Hazleck's avarice with a vengeance. He denied the accusation and, to his surprise, he was believed.

'There is of course another way,' Hazleck said quietly. He thought for a moment. 'Yes, I could get back the dark youth for nothing and it would necessitate a little bonus in that you would also have to be free . . . Stay there.'

He left the cubicle and Denton waited. He was sure the slippery old rogue would manage to do what he said.

The brothel keeper was furious. He stormed into the cubicle and pulled Denton to his feet.

'You think you can trick me?' he raged. 'What do you people have against honest men whose only crime is to try to make a living? I have kept an orderly house and I don't relish dealing with the likes of Hazleck. What am I supposed to do?'

Denton was taken aback. He wished Hazleck had made him privy to whatever lie he had told, then at least they could have got their story straight. He looked for Hazleck, but he was not there.

'I can't say anything,' he said. This at least was true, but it sounded lame even so.

'Was I to know you were an Elder? Or that other boy was your lover? I know what all this is about: you trick me into buying you so you can fulfil your secret desires at my expense. Then, when you've had enough, your fellows come in here and have me arrested for making a whore out of one of their number. I would be arrested! Kidnapping an Elder! Why, I would never see freedom again!'

'Your slaves are not free,' said Denton simply. The trick had worked after all. He would never have thought of it. Hazleck, he decided, was a genius.

'Leave my house!' The man's rage abated slightly. 'Please,

leave me in peace. I mean you no harm. I only want to make a living.'

Clothes were brought and Denton was shown out of the building. Before he left, he dictated that the slave Ghani should be given his freedom. His condition was agreed and he stepped into the Illyrian sunset, a free man once more.

'I have business in Tarne,' he told Hazleck, who was anxious to get back to the inn where Sanjha awaited him. 'I must have money for my journey. You can afford some, I hope?'

'Parting with money is worse than parting with a lover,' Hazleck returned. 'Yes, I will give you enough to get you there. There's a boat sailing any time now. They will be at the mainland before nightfall.'

Meanwhile, at Tarne, Morgan had noticed Caspar was not his usual ebullient self. The Night of Orion had arrived. He had secured his sacrificial victim – that in itself should have put him in a good mood. Moreover, the vexing figure of Denton was, thanks to Morgan, now reduced to being a slave, with his enquiries having yielded nothing. Despite all this, Caspar seemed tired and preoccupied.

Morgan, on the other hand, was more confident these days. It was because of him the community was safe once again. He had none of Leon's weak-willed notions of kindness towards the men they owned. Morgan was leadership material and he was sure Caspar would soon honour him above Leon. In any case, neither he nor Caspar could be altogether sure of that man's trustworthiness. Morgan had no evidence of course. If he had, he would have thought nothing of making sure his colleague suffered the same fate as Denton. It was annoying not to be able to prove his misgivings. He would have dearly loved to have Leon stripped, chained and sold to the disagreeable Hazleck. Part of this desire came from Morgan's deep love of seeing Leon naked. Morgan had always found Leon's debonair manner attractive. Recognising this, and not liking it one bit, he had dismissed any feelings of tenderness in favour of a carnal aspiration to have that lovely, hairy body bound and scourged.

Caspar had sent for him. Morgan was confident he would leave the interview with good news or some special reward for his services. Normally, nobody would be allowed in Caspar's rooms, certainly not without his permission. Morgan thought this a conceit and would have considered himself to be above such rules had Caspar not, on one memorable occasion, singled him out and told him especially. He would have liked Leon to know he was about to be favoured, but Leon was nowhere about and time was pressing.

Morgan knocked at the door and waited for permission to enter. He had made Cuthwin lick the sweat from his body beforehand. He preferred this to bathing: it made him feel good and it reminded Cuthwin of his abject place in the world. He had considered fucking his slave but had decided against it. Instead, he'd left Cuthwin hanging by his wrists from an overhead beam. He would deal with him later.

He was told to enter. Caspar was lying on his bed, his gown loosely wrapped about him. He was handsome, Morgan knew it, and he hated him for it. Even with the growing evidence of stress on his features, Caspar looked ravishing. Caspar told Morgan to sit on the bed beside him and he sighed.

'All is not well,' he said.

Morgan's hopes vanished. Caspar had summoned him only to give him some other tiresome duty. It was probably to do with the two slaves they had punished earlier. Was he to cut them down already? Or did they have to be dispensed with? Usually, this meant another trip to Hazleck's ship. Caspar had decreed they should never spill human blood unless it was on the altar.

'If only I could have some peace!' Caspar shouted suddenly. Then, more quietly, he said, 'The spirits are not satisfied with

195

our work. They need more from us before they will accept our offering. What I have to do is difficult for me and you must not question it. Do you agree?'

'I do,' Morgan replied.

'I have sent for Leon also. He will be here shortly. He must witness what is to happen so all who stand at the altar will have been part of it.'

Morgan tried to hide his anger. It was always the same. Why did Caspar allow Leon these privileges?

'If it must happen that way, it must,' was all he said.

Caspar smiled thinly. 'I know, I know. You don't understand. You couldn't be expected to. I follow ancient prophecies and I must be obedient to them. Leon is part of us, even if our instincts might tell us otherwise. Why else do you think I had him promoted so soon after his arrival here?'

Not for the first time, Morgan doubted the veracity of Caspar's dialogue with the occult world. He couldn't say this in so many words, but he could raise a metaphoric eyebrow.

'I'm sure you have your reasons,' he said.

Caspar was in no mood for implied sarcasm. His impatience boiled over into rage.

'Why must you always question me? Have you any idea what you're talking about? I think not. If you doubt me after tonight is over, you're no longer fit to serve with me.'

'After tonight?' Morgan queried. 'Why is tonight so special?'

'I don't want this, but I must do it,' Caspar said wearily. 'The spirits have told me I must be stripped, my hands and feet bound and I must be fucked.' He said this without emotion, but his hands were trembling. 'I must be fucked by you,' he finished.

Morgan's amazement almost matched the surge of greedy desire. He had to hide his delight and pretend duty. He just about manged it.

'If it must be, I will do it.'

Leon's footsteps approached and, when he entered the room,

he too was told what was to happen. To Morgan's great pleasure, Leon was to have no active part in it. He was there to watch.

Caspar produced some rope and a small plate on which there was ointment and a sheath. He stood by the foot of the bed.

'Take my gown from me and bind me across my chest with my hands tied at the wrists in front.'

Morgan did this, all the time fearing he would be stopped. Caspar had his eyes closed. His cock was rigid – this was not so much of a trial as Caspar was pretending it to be.

Leon had said virtually nothing. He sat away from them, looking on with interest, but apparently not wishing to be involved further.

When he had been trussed according to his instructions Caspar knelt on the floor, his arse towards Morgan.

'You mustn't be naked. Just take your cock out of your trousers and fuck me.'

Morgan hesitated. He wanted to take over now. He suspected this was no ritual – a fantasy of Caspar's perhaps. He liked that idea. Caspar desired him and needed a fuck. How else would he do it without losing his dignity?

Caspar, even when naked and bound, could still command by force of his personality. 'Do it!' he shouted. 'Do it, now! Fuck me!'

Morgan's cock was soon wrapped in the clinging, thin sheath. He always enjoyed experiencing the sensuous qualities of this veneer. He ran his finger over the smooth surface. Soon his prick would be further encased inside the most powerful man he had ever met. If only he could be allowed to use him properly. It wasn't right for the man he was fucking to have control. He wondered how Caspar would respond to a few harsh words and maybe a light beating. Morgan couldn't bring himself to attempt it.

He rubbed ointment on Caspar's arse and used the rest to lubricate his own prick. Then he knelt behind and entered.

Caspar let out a long hiss as the cock went up him.

'Take it easily. I have never had any other man inside me. I'm not one of the slaves.'

Morgan found it difficult to be careful with his cock. He pushed in very gradually, but he could tell Caspar was still hurting. Morgan rested where he was, half in. If Caspar could get used to that, he might be able to go further.

'Yes, that's starting to ease. Move your cock out very slowly and put it back this far.'

Morgan did as he was told. Caspar had loosened his muscles and, this time, Morgan was able almost to go full length. Caspar's uneasy breathing guided him: when there was a sharp intake of breath, he knew he must rest.

'I'm there,' Caspar said at last. 'Now, you can do it. Remember this, you won't have it again. Be grateful for it.'

Morgan fucked him, but not in the usual, savage way he fucked Cuthwin. He took his time and was mindful of giving pleasure as well as receiving it. His come did not rush out of his prick at all once: over before he knew it. It warmed inside his balls, ebbing and flowing towards the head of his penis until it could do so no more. He had never known the throbbing completeness of true lovemaking. A groan erupted from his stomach in time with the long, glowing orgasm. It was wonderful to him and he was weak with it.

Caspar told him to pull out, but to leave him tied until he had come himself. Morgan wanked him carefully. He took note of Caspar's every little movement, slowing down or quickening the pace as they dictated. In less than a minute, Caspar's breast began to heave and he strained in his bonds. Semen splattered over Morgan's hand. It was over.

Once himself again, Caspar spoke to the two of them in his customary, mysterious way. Morgan was still not persuaded, but he knew better than to interrupt.

'Three people have been among us. I recognised the omen

and I have guarded against it. One of the three is the slave, Troy. He will be our offering and it is right that it should be so. Once he is gone, the others have no power. The remaining two are here because of him, yet none of them have ever met. It was told at the beginning this would happen. We must be guarded, but with confidence now. Without the last part of the prophecy we are safe from them.'

'The last part?' Leon asked. 'What is that?'

Caspar turned to him. 'Your presence has also been foretold. Your face was shown to me in a vision. They said you are the man who will save Tarne from its greatest danger. I have treated you well, haven't I? You will be there for us?'

Leon nodded carefully. He was either trying to make sense of the words or, like Morgan, he was beginning to think Caspar was crazed in some way.

'If I am to do it, I must know the last part of the prophecy,' he said at last.

Caspar seemed fearful all of a sudden. He dropped his voice. 'My family are mostly hateful to me,' he said. 'Not just because they are arrogant and stupid, but because it is said the Lord of Tarne, my ancestor, will always be safe unless he is challenged by another of the same blood. If these three people have come to us, so must another. My brother, gentlemen. We must guard ourselves against my brother.'

Pascal

We had spent the night in Leon's rooms. He had put our legs in irons, but had not locked them. If anyone had come in unexpectedly, we were to say we had been brought there to be fucked by him later.

We couldn't sleep. What Leon had told us was unbelieveable and yet it had to be true. I took comfort in my instinct that good would always prevail over evil, but all the same, I was nervous. We might be discovered at any point and I didn't doubt this would mean our deaths.

André had been given the choice of staying with me or being left where he was. There, if all went according to our plan, he would be collected by me later. If it didn't, he wouldn't have been implicated in any further wrongdoing. But he was having none of this. He had sworn he would never desert me.

'But I can't expect you to risk your life,' I told him. 'You're a victim of Tarne. You haven't asked to be part of any of this. Had it not been for your bad luck in being punished by Caspar on the very day I was brought to the place, you might never have even spoken to me.'

'We would have found each other,' he said gently and sincerely. He kissed my cheek and ran the back of his hand lovingly over the place where his lips had touched my skin. 'In any case, I would willingly go through my whole life again without changing a jot of it, if it meant I found my way back to being tied to that tree with you before me for the first time. If I haven't asked to be part of your danger, I am happy to be so.'

I, on the other hand, had chosen all this, albeit unwittingly. Now I was too much taken with my own sense of adventure to deny Leon what he had asked of me. To tell the truth, it made me feel important.

I had listened with an accelerating thrill as Leon had explained it all. It was amazing to be told someone long ago had predicted these events. There had been nothing that had deviated from what Caspar's ancestor had seen and written about. In no act of mine, not even a small one, had my free will been given precedence over what fate had intended for me.

One day (at a party as it happened, though I'm sure our meeting would have taken place elsewhere in the same way), it had been seen that I would speak to a man from the family of Tarne. He would be able to recognise me from his own great-grandfather's supernatural prophecy and I would follow him. Even my attraction to Troy had been foretold. Troy, who was now in peril of his life.

The dark forces could try to swamp the village of Tarne completely. I was strong enough to join the few who were a force for good. We would take them on and bring tyranny to an end.

I blush now to think of this heroic nonsense. It all seems far away – a long time ago. Sometimes, with other events in my life, my memory dodges behind the years, appearing back briefly in different guises, but the events at Tarne are as sharp and clear as if they had happened yesterday.

★ ★ ★

André wanked me as we lay together. I was still worried: he might rather we had taken Leon's alternative offer and escaped. I was torn between my protective love for André and my duty to rescue Troy.

If I was one of the people who had to be there to break this curse, then I had no choice but to go. Even though Leon would not force me to risk my life, it would be a poor life left to me if I ran away now. André insisted he understood this and, equally, he refused to leave my side.

At the appointed hour, we rose and clothed ourselves in the garments Leon had left for us. It was near to daybreak. We had two knives with us and a map which Leon had sketched. Even with its help, it might have been difficult to find our way through the corridors had it not been for André's animal-like sense of direction.

A long tunnel lay before us. At its other end would be the hill where, according to Leon, Troy would have only recently been taken. We stumbled along in the darkness. Feeble light strained towards us, reaching into the blackness but too weak to permeate it. We knew we were nearing the outside world.

We hid in the bushes and watched. In the near distance we could see the altar and the strange figures that surrounded it. The sun was behind us, still low in the sky, but its rays filtered through the trees growing stronger very gradually.

Caspar prepared a fire on to which he cast some incense. The other two, Morgan and Leon, stood close by. All three were robed in white. They gave no indication of having heard our approach. I thought Leon looked across several times, but the light was still dim and it was impossible to be sure.

Since Leon had revealed his purpose at Tarne, I realised I could no longer split my desire between him and André. Leon's buccaneer attitude had been assumed. He was in reality, a quiet, lovely man. He had the potential to be a master. I had experienced this first when I had been his special slave. He would have had me believe this too was bluff. He hadn't been sure I was the one he sought and he couldn't risk my suspicion. It was possible, but I wondered whether his denial was more for his own benefit. He had seen the dreadful possibilities of his predilections and he feared them.

Maybe the supernatural was still at work, this time allowing me a glimpse into the future. I knew already where his affections would find their home.

Troy lay on the altar. He was secured at its four corners, and his eyes were covered, but he was otherwise naked. His young body was arched slightly – they'd put something under his back to force his cock and balls upward. I guessed this was for no other purpose than to humiliate him. The sight brought back my righteous anger: Caspar could have almost any man he wanted and yet he chose, in these degrading, deranged ceremonies, to use unwilling victims.

André sensed my thoughts and, to show his empathy, took my hand in his. He brushed his lips against my cheek.

'There is a part of all of us which would do the same,' he answered. 'This boy, Troy, has been forced and that is what is wicked. But the ceremony itself is no more evil than those in which we have often been more than eager to take our own part.'

'Not with a knife at our throats,' I reminded him.

'No,' he said softly. 'Not that.'

There had to be another man with us before the prophecy would be able to come full circle. Leon had told us we had no power to bring this person's presence about. He knew who it was: a prisoner called Denton who had been sold by Morgan. Leon had traced the merchant who had taken him. Incredibly, the trader had sworn Denton had been set free and was, even then, on his way back to the mainland.

'We must trust and hope,' Leon had said. 'It seems the gods are smiling on us: from what I have heard, Hazleck freeing a slave is an apocalyptic event in itself. Denton is being guided towards us. Not one of us is anything more than a piece on a board. We will be moved into the correct places when the time is right.'

The dawn was breaking. This was surely the moment to do something, but what? All three of the Superiors stripped themselves. They were erect, even Leon. We watched as Caspar mounted and buried his cock in between Troy's firm buttocks. Caspar proceeded to fuck him and I felt my hatred boiling inside me.

Troy's anal passage must have been desensitised from having been taken so many times the night before. He was groaning under the weight of the other man, but he had given no sharp cry as Caspar had entered him. Morgan climbed up by his head and made Troy suck his cock. All this while, Leon was glancing anxiously towards the sun. I knew he was looking for something – anything – that might signify it was time to act.

My foot caught on a branch and it rustled the bush that concealed us. Morgan looked directly towards me, but he must have presumed the disturbance to come from some animal and he paid it no heed.

Caspar was almost at his climax: I could tell from the frantic movements of his hips and the way he threw his head back. His hands were on Troy's chest, twisting his nipples. Morgan appeared to be engrossed in the sight of Caspar's body as a voyeur might have been. He was rubbing his thick cock, shoving it into Troy's mouth only every so often and without so much as a glance at their prisoner. His face was directed fully towards Caspar and I could make out some of his words as they carried on the morning breeze:

'That's right. Fuck his arse! Let him have your spunk before he is taken by these spirits of yours. Let him have it!'

Then everything began to happen almost at once.

Morgan, himself now close to orgasm, began to gasp. 'Yes, that's good. I'll have you again, Caspar, you bastard! I'll fuck you again tonight! I'll take your arse!'

Caspar stopped abruptly and pulled out of Troy's arse.

'You dare to say that?' he screamed. 'You dare?'

He grabbed Morgan and they struggled together over Troy's helpless body. Morgan was pleading with Caspar even though, as the stronger of the two men, he had the advantage and was able to hold Caspar at bay.

Leon took his chance. While the other two fought, he was able to free one of Troy's hands. Morgan saw him and shouted as much over Caspar's stream of furious curses. Caspar, too bent on doing Morgan physical injury to pay him any heed, managed to break free and attack him once again. Morgan avoided the blow and tried to reach Leon. Caspar, seeing nothing of this intent, leapt on top of both of them and began pounding away with his fists.

'This is it,' I said to André. 'We have to do it now.'

I ran towards them and, using my knife, cut Troy free. Then I joined in the fray, tackling Morgan while Leon took on Caspar.

Morgan was immensely strong and I was no match for him. Within a few moments, he had the knife out of my hand and was holding it to my throat. André came up behind him and locked Morgan's neck in a stranglehold. The knife fell and I grabbed it.

'No!' Leon shouted. 'Not yet!'

Troy, dazed and weary, was able to stagger over to us,

bringing the ropes that had bound him. I wound them round Morgan's body as he spluttered and swore.

Caspar was, by now, lying flat on his back with Leon astride him. Leon was pushing down on his face and Caspar's hands were gripped round Leon's neck.

'You can't do it!' Caspar screamed. 'You're part of all this. You are here to save Tarne, not to destroy it!'

'To save it, yes,' Leon gasped. 'But to save it from you. You've had it all wrong Caspar. I am the one who is come to destroy you!'

'Only one of my blood can do that . . . The prophecy . . .'

Another man had come running towards us. He was older than we were, but strikingly handsome. He wore the clothes of a sailor, but his slender frame belied his costume. His hair was glowing in the red of the sunrise, a deep-brown colour. He wasn't a Superior of Tarne. My hopes rose: this must be the one we were waiting for.

'Join hands with me,' Leon shouted.

I glanced at André. 'Not you,' I said. 'You've done all you can. I love you.'

I stole a brief kiss from my lover and grabbed the stranger's hand in mine – and Troy's on the other side.

'Do as he says,' I screamed to Troy. 'Quickly!'

The day was almost fully upon us. Troy took Leon's hand. At the same moment, a cloud passed over the sun. Morgan was still struggling for freedom, but André was guarding him. Leon raised his knife.

'I am of your blood,' he said to Caspar. 'Your father is my father, though I never knew him. I am here to save Tarne.'

The cloud burst over us. Rain drenched our bodies, but we hardly noticed it. Leon plunged the knife into Caspar's throat.

★　★　★

Caspar writhed on the ground like a serpent that had been cut in two. His face grew old before our eyes. Wrinkles spread like weeds over his skin and his hair became white, then it fell away from his scalp. His hands clutched at the air. They had become the hands of an old, old man. His expression was of pure malevolence. He was saying something but we couldn't make out the words. He gripped Leon's throat.

At first, his grip was powerful, but within seconds, years passed over his body and his grasp weakened. He fell back.

He lay still with the rain washing over his face. His expression smoothed and the Caspar we knew gradually took over once again. The horror we had just witnessed and even the wound on his throat were washed off him as though they were no more than superficial dirt.

The heavy rain turned into a shower and then into a light drizzle.

The sun rose and Caspar opened his eyes.

Epilogue

The village of Tarne is now a different place.

Denton lives close to the tavern where he still visits with his lover, Cuthwin. Troy, who it transpired was the object of Denton's mission in Tarne, has never gone back to his parents. Until they accept Leon as his partner, he swears he will not see them again.

Morgan was excused his crimes. His repentance may have been brought about by force, but I am sure he is a coward at heart. He had seen what we had seen: his fear of devils at which he'd previously scoffed would always hold him in check.

André and I are still as deeply in love as we were then. He is still subservient, but I hope I have taught him to respect himself. He gives his body to me because he wants to. If I choose to have him in chains, it is because they make him the more beautiful. If he wants this situation to be reversed, he tells me so, and I am ready to strip off my clothes and feel his whip across my back. Its kisses are necessary to me once every while. I am not ashamed any more than he is himself.

★ ★ ★

We were once visited by a plump, cheerful merchant and his lover. Denton asked us to join them in the tavern.

The older man was a surprising choice for the young, dark youth who never left his side. Hazleck – for that was his name – told us he'd been a slave-trader, but now declared he had no taste for it.

'I deal in clothes,' he explained. 'I love clothes, don't you?'

His epicene manner was not to my tastes but, later, André claimed he'd found it endearing.

'If Sanjha has chosen him, he must have qualities we do not see. We must not allow our own tastes to cloud our judgments of others.'

André is always like this: wise and sometimes gently reproving. It transpired Hazleck had had more than a small part to play in our own adventures, though no mention was made of him in Caspar's prophecy. When this was mentioned, he had squeezed Sanjha's hand with his gold-laden fingers and smiled.

'We were mere pawns, my dears. We didn't know. If we had, I doubt it would have made any difference. It seems what must happen must happen. We can do little to prevent it.'

I was sure he was right. One day, André and I will sail over to Illyria and take up his offer of hospitality. Without Hazleck, we would not have had Denton and, without Denton's presence, we might not now have each other.

And what of Caspar?

He didn't remember who he was or how he'd come to be lying on the grass in a place he claimed was completely new to him.

We had taken him back to Tarne. Leon had insisted on binding him, though I was beginning to doubt this precaution was needed.

He now lives in the house where I first visited him and, as far as I know, he is still a single man with his life before him.

One might suppose his memories would haunt him, but I believe those memories belong to another person.

I speak, of course, of Caspar's great-grandfather: a man who cheated Death itself by inhabiting the bodies of other men and stealing from them the years that had been denied him. The souls he had taken in his name will now have peace.

The story of the Lord of Tarne has been told often. Each time details change and now I scarcely recognise it as something that happened to me. Those of us who were there do not discuss it. I have been persuaded to set my pen to paper at last. This is the truth of it and I am content to let it rest.

IDOL NEW BOOKS

Also published:

THE KING'S MEN
Christian Fall

Ned Medcombe, spoilt son of an Oxfordshire landowner, has always remembered his first love: the beautiful, golden-haired Lewis. But seventeenth-century England forbids such a love and Ned is content to indulge his domineering passions with the willing members of the local community, including the submissive parish cleric. Until the Civil War changes his world, and he is forced to pursue his desires as a soldier in Cromwell's army – while his long-lost lover fights as one of the King's men.

ISBN 0 352 33207 7

THE VELVET WEB
Christopher Summerisle

The year is 1889. Daniel McGaw arrives at Calverdale, a centre of academic excellence buried deep in the English countryside. But this is like no other college. As Daniel explores, he discovers secret passages in the grounds and forbidden texts in the library. The young male students, isolated from the outside world, share a darkly bizarre brotherhood based on the most extreme forms of erotic expression. It isn't long before Daniel is initiated into the rites that bind together the youths of Calverdale in a web of desire.

ISBN 0 352 33208 5

CHAINS OF DECEIT
Paul C. Alexander

Journalist Nathan Dexter's life is turned around when he meets a young student called Scott – someone who offers him the relationship for which he's been searching. Then Nathan's best friend goes missing, and Nathan uncovers evidence that he has become the victim of a slavery ring which is rumoured to be operating out of London's leather scene. To rescue their friend and expose the perverted slave trade, Nathan and Scott must go undercover, risking detection and betrayal at every turn.

ISBN 0 352 33206 9

HALL OF MIRRORS
Robert Black

Tom Jarrett operates the Big Wheel at Gamlin's Fair. When young runaway Jason Bradley tries to rob him, events are set in motion which draw the two together in a tangled web of mutual mistrust and growing fascination. Each carries a burden of old guilt and tragic unspoken history; each is running from something. But the fair is a place of magic and mystery where normal rules don't apply, and Jason is soon on a journey of self-discovery, unbridled sexuality and growing love.

ISBN 0 352 33209 3

THE SLAVE TRADE
James Masters

Barely eighteen and innocent of the desires of men, Marc is the sole survivor of a noble British family. When his home village falls to the invading Romans, he is forced to flee for his life. He first finds sanctuary with Karl, a barbarian from far-off Germanica, whose words seem kind but whose eyes conceal a dark and brooding menace. And then they are captured by Gaius, a general in Caesar's all-conquering army, in whose camp they learn the true meaning – and pleasures – of slavery.

ISBN 0 352 33228 X

DARK RIDER
Jack Gordon

While the rulers of a remote Scottish island play bizarre games of sexual dominance with the Argentinian Angelo, his friend Robert – consumed with jealous longing for his coffee-skinned companion – assuages his desires with the willing locals.

ISBN 0 352 33243 3

CONQUISTADOR
Jeff Hunter

It is the dying days of the Aztec empire. Axaten and Quetzel are members of the Stable, servants of the Sun Prince chosen for their bravery and beauty. But it is not just an honour and a duty to join this society, it is also the ultimate sexual achievement. Until the arrival of Juan, a young Spanish conquistador, sets the men of the Stable on an adventure of bondage, lust and deception.

ISBN 0 352 33244 1

WE NEED YOUR HELP . . .
to plan the future of Idol books –

Yours are the only opinions that matter. Idol is a new and exciting venture: the first British series of books devoted to homoerotic fiction for men.

We're going to do our best to provide the sexiest, best-written books you can buy. And we'd like you to help in these early stages. Tell us what you want to read. There's a freepost address for your filled-in questionnaires, so you won't even need to buy a stamp.

THE IDOL QUESTIONNAIRE

SECTION ONE: ABOUT YOU

1.1 Sex (*we presume you are male, but just in case*)
Are you?
      Male   ☐
      Female   ☐

1.2 Age
      under 21   ☐   21–30   ☐
      31–40   ☐   41–50   ☐
      51–60   ☐   over 60 ☐

1.3 At what age did you leave full-time education?
      still in education ☐   16 or younger ☐
      17–19   ☐   20 or older   ☐

1.4 Occupation _____

1.5 Annual household income _____

1.6 We are perfectly happy for you to remain anonymous; but if you would
     like us to send you a free booklist of Idol books, please insert your name
     and address

     _____

     _____

     _____

     _____

SECTION TWO: ABOUT BUYING IDOL BOOKS

2.1 Where did you get this copy of *Slaves of Tarne*?
     Bought at chain book shop   ☐
     Bought at independent book shop   ☐
     Bought at supermarket   ☐
     Bought at book exchange or used book shop   ☐
     I borrowed it/found it   ☐
     My partner bought it   ☐

2.2 How did you find out about Idol books?
     I saw them in a shop   ☐
     I saw them advertised in a magazine   ☐
     I read about them in _____
     Other _____

2.3 Please tick the following statements if you agree with them:
     I would be less embarrassed about buying Idol
        books if the cover pictures were less explicit   ☐
     I think that in general the pictures on Idol
        books are about right   ☐
     I think Idol cover pictures should be as
        explicit as possible   ☐

2.4 Would you read an Idol book in a public place – on a train for instance?
     Yes   ☐   No   ☐

SECTION THREE: ABOUT THIS IDOL BOOK

3.1 Do you think the sex content in this book is:
     Too much   ☐   About right   ☐
     Not enough   ☐

3.2 Do you think the writing style in this book is:
   Too unreal/escapist ☐   About right ☐
   Too down to earth ☐

3.3 Do you think the story in this book is:
   Too complicated ☐   About right ☐
   Too boring/simple ☐

3.4 Do you think the cover of this book is:
   Too explicit ☐   About right ☐
   Not explicit enough ☐

Here's a space for any other comments:

SECTION FOUR: ABOUT OTHER IDOL BOOKS

4.1 How many Idol books have you read?

4.2 If more than one, which one did you prefer?

4.3 Why?

SECTION FIVE: ABOUT YOUR IDEAL EROTIC NOVEL

We want to publish the books you want to read – so this is your chance to tell us exactly what your ideal erotic novel would be like.

5.1 Using a scale of 1 to 5 (1 = no interest at all, 5 = your ideal), please rate the following possible settings for an erotic novel:
   Roman / Ancient World ☐
   Medieval / barbarian / sword 'n' sorcery ☐
   Renaissance / Elizabethan / Restoration ☐
   Victorian / Edwardian ☐
   1920s & 1930s ☐
   Present day ☐
   Future / Science Fiction ☐

5.2 Using the same scale of 1 to 5, please rate the following themes you may find in an erotic novel:

> Bondage / fetishism ☐
> Romantic love ☐
> SM / corporal punishment ☐
> Bisexuality ☐
> Group sex ☐
> Watersports ☐
> Rent / sex for money ☐

5.3 Using the same scale of 1 to 5, please rate the following styles in which an erotic novel could be written:

> Gritty realism, down to earth ☐
> Set in real life but ignoring its more unpleasant aspects ☐
> Escapist fantasy, but just about believable ☐
> Complete escapism, totally unrealistic ☐

5.4 In a book that features power differentials or sexual initiation, would you prefer the writing to be from the viewpoint of the dominant / experienced or submissive / inexperienced characters:

> Dominant / Experienced ☐
> Submissive / Inexperienced ☐
> Both ☐

5.5 We'd like to include characters close to your ideal lover. What characteristics would your ideal lover have? Tick as many as you want:

Dominant	☐	Caring	☐
Slim	☐	Rugged	☐
Extroverted	☐	Romantic	☐
Bisexual	☐	Old	☐
Working class	☐	Intellectual	☐
Introverted	☐	Professional	☐
Submissive	☐	Pervy	☐
Cruel	☐	Ordinary	☐
Young	☐	Muscular	☐
Naïve	☐		

Anything else? _____

5.6 Is there one particular setting or subject matter that your ideal erotic novel would contain:

_____

5.7 As you'll have seen, we include safe-sex guidelines in every book. However, while our policy is always to show safe sex in stories with contemporary settings, we don't insist on safe-sex practices in stories with historical settings because it would be anachronistic. What, if anything, would you change about this policy?

_____

_____

SECTION SIX: LAST WORDS

6.1 What do you like best about Idol books?

_____

6.2 What do you most dislike about Idol books?

_____

6.3 In what way, if any, would you like to change Idol covers?

_____

6.4 Here's a space for any other comments:

_____

_____

_____

_____

Thanks for completing this questionnaire. Now either tear it out, or photocopy it, then put it in an envelope and send it to:

Idol
FREEPOST
London
W10 5BR

You don't need a stamp if you're in the UK, but you'll need one if you're posting from overseas.